"Hunter...don't."

He ought to heed the warning, but couldn't. "Don't what?"

Claire pursed her lips. "You know *what!*"

Inside, he ached to laugh. Claire Dent didn't pout very often, but when she did it was the prettiest little pout this side of the Mississippi. Reluctantly, Hunter released her.

"I just needed a 'Welcome back home.' And," he admitted, "maybe a little hug."

"I'm not the one to offer it, Hunter. We both know that."

"Claire, the first half of my life you were my best friend. I don't want to spend the last half of my life thinking I've made you my enemy."

"I'm not your enemy," she denied. "I just want to walk out of this awkward situation with some class, that's all."

"Fine. I'll let you," he said. "But before you walk out that door, let's resolve our hard feelings. I say we kiss and make up."

Dear Reader,

From hardworking singles to loving sisters, this month's books are filled with lively, engaging heroines offering you an invitation into the world of Silhouette Romance...where fairy tales really do come true!

Arabia comes to America in the sultry, seductive *Engaged to the Sheik* (SR #1750) by Sue Swift, the fourth tale of the spellbinding IN A FAIRY TALE WORLD... miniseries. When a matchmaking princess leads a sexy sheik and a chic city girl into a fake engagement, tempers—and sparks—are sure to fly. Don't miss a moment of the magic!

All work is lots of fun when you're falling for the boss— and his adorable baby girl! Raye Morgan launches her BOARDROOM BRIDES miniseries with *The Boss, the Baby and Me* (SR #1751) in which a working girl discovers the high-powered exec she *thought* was a snake in the grass is actually the man of her dreams.

Twin sisters are supposed to help each other out. So when her glamorous business-minded sister gets cold feet, this staid schoolteacher agrees to switch places—as the bride! Will becoming *The Substitute Fiancée* (SR #1752) lead to happily ever after? Find out in this romantic tale from Rebecca Russell.

Rediscover the miracle of forgiveness in the latest book from DeAnna Talcott, *A Ring and a Rainbow* (SR #1753). As childhood sweethearts they'd promised each other forever, but that was a long time ago. Can these two adults get past their heartbreak to face the reality of a life together?

Sincerely,

Mavis C. Allen
Associate Senior Editor

Please address questions and book requests to:
Silhouette Reader Service
U.S.: 3010 Walden Ave., P.O. Box 1325, Buffalo, NY 14269
Canadian: P.O. Box 609, Fort Erie, Ont. L2A 5X3

A Ring and a Rainbow

DeANNA TALCOTT

SILHOUETTE *Romance*®

Published by Silhouette Books

America's Publisher of Contemporary Romance

To my father,
whose keen mind and limitless imagination
allowed him to see every possibility.

 SILHOUETTE BOOKS

ISBN 0-373-19753-5

A RING AND A RAINBOW

Copyright © 2005 by DeAnna Talcott

Visit Silhouette Books at www.eHarlequin.com

Printed in U.S.A.

Books by DeAnna Talcott

Silhouette Romance

The Cowboy and the Christmas Tree #1125
The Bachelor and the Bassinet #1189
To Wed Again? #1206
The Triplet's Wedding Wish #1370
Marrying for a Mom #1543
The Nanny & Her Scrooge #1568
Her Last Chance #1628
Cupid Jones Gets Married #1646
Fill-In Fiancée #1694
A Ring and a Rainbow #1753

DeANNA TALCOTT

grew up in rural Nebraska, where her love of reading was fostered in a one-room school. It was there she first dreamed of writing the kinds of books that would touch people's hearts. Her dream became a reality. In her writing career, DeAnna has earned the National Reader's Choice Award, the Holt Medallion, the WISRWA Write-Touch Readers Choice Award and the Booksellers' Best Award for the best traditional romance. All of her award-winning books have been Silhouette Romance titles!

DeAnna claims a retired husband and three children make her life in mid-Michigan particularly interesting. When not writing, or talking about writing, she scrounges flea markets for vintage toys, attends sporting events and fosters adoptable puppies for occasional weekends away from the animal shelter.

THE LEGEND OF THE DOUBLE RAINBOW

One day the skies parted and an unknown hand drizzled colors of unfathomable brilliance in a wide, sweeping arc. The people wondered at such beauty and gaped in awe at the masterpiece.

Each color soon became known for a virtue, hope or expectation. Red for passion, yellow for inspiration, orange for courage, green for prosperity, blue for love, violet for beauty. None of the colors could stand alone—yet together they appeared indomitable, and even as they faded away they heralded a new lush life of warmth and promise. The people named these colors the rainbow and knew that when the rainbow touched the earth goodness would flow into the soil and bless those who discovered the rainbow's foothold.

Soon, the unknown hand painted a second sweeping arc across the heavens, creating two rainbows in a single sky!

From then on, those who witnessed such a rare event discovered riches of the body and spirit that knew no bounds and could never, ever be stilled.

Prologue

"Rain's stopped," six-year-old Hunter Starnes announced.

Beside him, Claire Dent, five, huddled on the back stoop of the Starnes's cabin, her knees pulled up to her chest, her arms wrapped around her skinny legs.

Claire shrugged, and set her chin, fixing her gaze on the wispy dark clouds overhead. Momma and Daddy had been fighting again, and she guessed that was the reason they'd spent the afternoon at the cabin outside of town, talking to Hunter's mom. She'd heard Momma say Daddy had lost his job again, and Claire knew what that meant: She wouldn't be able to take treats to school next week for her birthday, and she probably wouldn't get any presents, either. Her mother would mix water in the tomato soup instead of milk, and they'd have to start eating that pukey oatmeal again, instead of cereal.

Claire kept studying the skies, watching, waiting. "Look," she said suddenly, straightening. "A rainbow."

"So? Last time we saw a double one." Hunter started picking at a scab on his knee, as if he didn't care about some silly old rainbow.

"You s'pose there's really a pot of gold at the end of the rainbow, Hunter?"

"I dunno. Maybe." He stopped picking and looked up, out of the corner of his eye.

"If we found a pot of gold, what would you do with it?"

"Me? Heck," he swore, wiping his hands on his shorts, "I'd buy everybody in Lost Falls ice cream. And you and me? We'd share one of those big sundaes with all the whipped cream and cherries and stuff. Twenty-seven scoops of ice cream. Just for us."

Claire smiled, thinking of it. "We'd have a party."

"Heck, yes. With balloons, and a band, and everything. And we'd invite everybody. Even that crabby Mrs. Harris."

Claire turned to look up at him, surprised. "You're not still mad at her?"

He shrugged. "Nah. I didn't mean to step on her stupid old flowers, no matter what she says. I mean, it was the only baseball we had. And since the rest of the guys were afraid to go in her backyard it was up to me to get it back."

"You're pretty brave. I wouldn't have done it. Not for nothin'," Claire said.

"Sometimes you gotta do what you gotta do. That's what my dad says."

Claire thought about that for a few moments. "If there was anything I ever felt like I had to do, it would be to make sure my Momma had a real nice house, and that she wasn't cryin' all the time. And I'd make my Daddy a doctor or somethin', so people looked up to him, and that way he'd always have a job."

Hunter looked at her, and his eyes went kind of soft, like

toffee that was melting in the sun. He slipped off the porch rail and came down to sit beside her on the steps. With one grimy hand, he awkwardly reached over to pat her bony knee. "Your daddy could be a doctor, Claire. If he wanted. Look how nice he stitched up Rufus, when he got hit by that car."

Claire nodded, and instead of thinking about how her father had sewn the jagged cut on Rufus's back leg, she fixed her gaze on the rainbow, vaguely wondering if wishing on it would be enough to make her dreams come true. Every time she was with Hunter, she thought she was the luckiest girl in the whole wide world. Last week she'd even gotten him to play "wedding" with her—even though he'd made her promise not to tell.

She'd worn her Grandma's long white fuzzy robe—the one that she'd dug out of the ragbag—and Hunter had worn the top hat that he'd gotten at the circus last year. Although they couldn't remember all the words, Hunter figured if they said the "till death do us part" stuff, that ought to do it.

Thinking back on it, Claire impulsively leaned over and gave Hunter a dry-lipped peck on the cheek.

"Yuck!" Hunter drew back and wiped at the spot. "Claire! Quit it! Girls don't go around kissing boys."

"I wasn't kissing boys," she said defensively. "I was kissing *you.*"

As if that made all the difference, Hunter forgot about it and sat back. The rainbow grew brighter, the colors more distinct. "Okay. Hey? You wanna find it?"

"What?"

"The gold at the end of the rainbow."

"You bet," Claire said, unconsciously echoing *her* daddy's favorite phrase.

Hunter bolted off the steps. "Finders keepers!" he yelled, racing ahead of her and into the woods.

Claire ran after him. They clambered over the split rail fence and scrambled through the thicket. They splashed through the creek and dashed over the sodden ground and into the field.

"Over there," Claire pointed. But when they looked up, the rainbow had dimmed.

They ran harder and faster, until Hunter held his side and Claire was out of breath.

"Wait. It's—it's gone…." she faltered, her face pinched.

They both looked at the place the rainbow was *supposed* to be and turned around—and around. Until they were dizzy, and they were certain it was gone.

"We waited too long," Hunter said finally. "Maybe next time."

There was nothing left to do but trudge back to the cabin.

"I thought for sure if we found it everybody would be happy," Claire said finally. She blinked back one hot tear before Hunter saw it and called her a crybaby. "At least for my mom and dad, and everything."

"You know, Claire," Hunter said, when they got to the fence, "I'll bet if we buried a little gold, the next time we had a double rainbow, it would make more. Lots more. And then all we'd have to do is just go dig it up, and we'd have all we'd ever need. We could do all the things we ever wanted to do. We could help everybody."

"Really?"

"Sure."

Claire stopped and looked at him, her eyes narrowing thoughtfully. "Hunter? I know where to get some gold."

"Yeah. Right."

"I do." She climbed over the fence and started walking faster. "Come on. I'll show you."

The car still stood in the driveway, and her mother's purse

was still in the front seat. Claire climbed in and zipped open the little side pocket. Then she pulled out the ring. "See. Momma showed me this morning. It was Grandma's. And it's real gold."

"Hey. Neat. That'll work. I'll get a can from the garbage and we'll bury it out in the woods. Nobody will ever find it but us." Hunter smiled widely, exposing a space where a tooth ought to be. "Claire, I'm telling you. We'll have everything we ever wanted. We're going to be rich. And we're going to make everybody happy."

Claire chose the deepest, darkest spot in the woods to bury the can, and as she patted the last handful of dirt atop it, had no idea that the only thing she was going to be was in trouble. Great big fat trouble.

Chapter One

In life there were supposed to be beginnings and endings, and when Claire Dent looked back over her thirty-four years in Lost Falls, Wyoming, she realized she'd had very few of either. Her life was like a story with a great big middle. It didn't have a particularly fascinating beginning, and it didn't appear to be heading toward any remarkable ending.

Today, however, changes were in the air.

If things went as she expected, she'd finally put "the end" on one of the most painful chapters of her life—and she'd be happy to do so.

She yanked open the oven door. She let 350 degrees of dry heat smash her in the face as she gazed in at the chicken pot pie. The gravy bubbled around the edges of a perfectly browned crust, and the scent was heavenly.

Heavenly.

Huh. What an ironic comparison to have, especially today. Claire had lived next door to Ella Starnes for as long as she could remember. The woman had been a paradox. As outspoken as a candidate on a bipartisan ballot, as charitable as a saint. It didn't seem possible that she was gone. She'd just slipped away in her sleep two nights ago. Of course, if there was a woman to make the heavens sing, it would be Ella. She was probably up there now, orchestrating some kind of plan.

Ella's oldest daughter, Beth, had called this morning, to tell Claire all the kids were coming home. There were five altogether. Beth, and her sisters—Mindy, Courtney, Lynda—and her brother, Hunter. Every one of the girls had married and moved away, yet they all came home at least once a year, sometimes more often. Claire knew their lives as intimately as she knew her own.

Hunter, on the other hand, was a different story. He hadn't found his way home in twelve years, and rumor had it that he was single, filthy rich and managing a reputation that alternated between reckless and restrained. Hunter was a venture capitalist, and Ella joked that he lost everyone's money but his own.

Claire could have cared less—but the idea of Hunter coming back rankled.

He was the last man on the face of the earth she ever wanted to see. Not *for* all these years, and not *after* all these years—and certainly not when she was messed up with grief about *his* mother. They'd parted ways when she refused to wait any longer for the wedding he'd promised her, and he insisted on going off to make something of himself. Their breakup was one notch short of ugly, but Claire had gone on about her business and held her head up—even though she knew everyone in town talked about how he'd jilted her.

Jilted, as in never a ring, only a promise.

Still, she had an obligation to the family, and as a good

neighbor, she'd see that obligation through. She'd take the pot pie over and leave it on the table so they could have a hot meal when they got in. She'd purposely avoid Hunter, even as she made him aware of her presence.

She'd let him know that here, in Lost Falls, people kept their promises to one another. That they ate pot pies, not beef Wellington and parsleyed potatoes.

It would be enough. For today.

Tomorrow, or the next day, or the day after that, he'd discover that she'd gotten him out of her system. He'd see first-hand that she wasn't impressed with him, or what he'd done with his life—or how much money he'd made. By the time it was all said and done she'd make sure he knew that she didn't regret staying in Lost Falls, not for one minute. In fact, by the time she was done, she'd make him wonder why he'd ever left.

Claire took out the pot pie and glanced out the side window. The kitchen windows of the Dent and Starnes homes faced each other, separated by a shared blacktop driveway. No one was home yet; the driveway was conspicuously empty.

She stepped outside, crossed the driveway, then hurried up the back-porch steps. Hesitating at the door, she fumbled with her key and balanced the hot dish. Ella's back-door lock had a personality all its own, and Claire had long ago learned to jiggle the key and pull it back before turning it. The lock turned, the hinges creaked and the door swung open.

Claire tiptoed in. Even though she'd been treated like part of the family for most of her life, stepping into the eerie, empty silence today made her feel like an intruder. Ella's coffee cup was beside the sink where she'd left it, and her favorite sweater hung over the back of a chair. Her reading glasses, bows crossed atop the weekly newspaper, still sat on the kitchen table, just as if she'd been reading and had left the room for her afternoon nap.

Yesterday, when the sheriff had called her over, Claire had debated putting some of the things away, but she'd chosen not to. It would be good for Ella's kids to feel their mother's presence in the house, just as she had. She knew from experience how hard it was to lose your mother, and she didn't want to take one thing away from them. Not one. No, she'd leave everything the way it was, and then they could do as they wished.

Ella's medicine bottles—including the one Claire had just had refilled for her on Friday—were clustered in the center of the table, looking more like condiments than prescriptions. Moving a couple of them back, Claire put the chicken pot pie on the table before slipping off the oven mitt. The writing pad and pencils were in the junk drawer, upper left, so she turned away to get them. Tearing off a sheet of paper from the lined tablet, she fished out a pencil.

The pencil was an old red one from the station. Starnes's Oil and Fuel. Let Us Take You Places. A rueful smile lifted the corner of her mouth. Huh. The only place it had ever taken her was to hell and back. She'd wasted half of her youth watching Hunter change oil filters, pump gas and wash windshields. She'd leaned over the hoods of the cars he'd tinkered with and listened to his dreams.

And never, not in a million years, had she ever considered that his dreams wouldn't include her. Nobody else had, either. Maybe that's why it had come as such a shock to both families when they'd broken up. It was the dreams he'd nurtured in college that had done them in. She'd had no idea someone's dreams could be that big, that consuming.

"Smells good. Very good."

Claire startled, as if she'd been shot from the sheer impact of the familiar honeyed voice. Her shoulder slammed against the wall, the pencil skittered from her grasp and rolled across the countertop.

"I…" Her explanation, as well as any rational thought, fled.

Hunter stood there in the doorway, barefoot, shirtless, the waist of his jeans sagging in a half-moon below his belly button. He had a white cotton T-shirt bunched in his fist, and his pose was edgy, as if he'd been ready to light into her.

Claire's heart hammered, her mouth went dry. His untimely entrance vaporized all the coolly polite greetings she had rehearsed. "You scared me," she accused.

"Didn't mean to." Hunter's burning gaze skimmed her, then dropped to the toes of her shoes and slowly worked its way back up.

Claire didn't wilt under the inspection and, strangely, she wasn't offended, either. She stared right back, returning the favor in full.

Damn him. He was everything she remembered and more. He was ruggedly handsome, and so masculine that, if measured, the virility quotient would likely pop the top off the charts. Why couldn't the man be stoop shouldered and paunchy, with glasses and a receding hairline?

But, no, that would have been too easy. No, he had to come back as a six-foot-four hardbody. At thirty-five, Hunter Starnes could live up to any trendy description and still manage to be a man's man. He was everything that filled her dreams and sleepless nights. Everything that haunted and teased her.

It surprised her a bit that he'd filled out, into the epitome of strength and resilience. He'd never looked like *this* at twenty.

The last decade had given him a sexier, bolder look. His face was wider, squarer. His forehead was broad and smooth, while smile lines bracketed his mouth, sculpting age and experience into the tanned expanse of his cheeks. The blunt curve of his jaw—and the sawed-off, notched chin—were sooty from a day's growth of stubble. It was the sort of look most women found mysteriously intoxicating—the look of a bad boy waiting to be tamed.

Most women. *Not her.*

And then there was his hair. Dark. Tousled. Sparse on the sides and decadently spiked. Clipped to precision, and trimmed to arch so perfectly over the flat shells of his ears that it made Claire realize he groomed his image just as much as he did his career.

His hazel eyes, which had always been flirty and fun, had subtly changed. Now a shrewd quality filled their depths, putting his expression somewhere between piercing and ponderous. It scared her a little and made her feel inexplicably vulnerable, as if he could see right down to the bottom of her soul. She saw a grief there, too…a grief that, this time around, she didn't know how to handle.

He still had the whitest, straightest teeth—and, she guessed, a mouth that occasionally twitched when he teased. A mouth she once knew as soft and sexy and seductively sinful when he kissed. A mouth that had once taught her about French kisses and hickies and the delicious rapid-fire rapport between men and women. Now his mouth was solemn, sad, the corners turned down.

If there was one compromise to perfection, it had to be his nose, she silently conceded, gratified to at least find something physically wrong with his looks. It still leaned a little off-kilter, his reward for playing smash-mouth basketball his senior year in high school.

"I meant it. Didn't mean to scare you, but—" he lifted an

eyebrow as well as an apologetic shoulder as he sauntered into the room, pausing at the edge of the kitchen table "—I wasn't expecting the girls yet, so I figured I ought to check out the noise, make sure no one broke in. I was ready to take you out."

"Sorry. I should have knocked," she said stiffly, straightening. Funny, the last time he'd suggested taking her out it had been for a *date*. "I'm so used to just coming over. But I wanted to leave dinner for your family, so it would be here when they got in." She didn't want him to think she'd made the meal solely for his benefit. She waggled the slip of paper. "I was going to leave a note, Hunter, along with my condolences."

His gaze narrowed, eyeing the blank sheet of paper as if it was an unsigned sympathy card. The muscle along his jaw tightened. "Thanks." The single word was rough, husky with unspent grief. "I appreciate it."

Claire hesitated, swallowing the lump in her throat. If he shed as much as one tear, she'd fall apart—and then she'd fall straight into his arms. "And I—I want you to know I'll miss your mom a lot."

He nodded, his eyes shuttering closed for the briefest of moments. His head tipped slightly forward, and then he drew a ragged breath. "Thanks, Claire. But…well…I imagine it was as much of a shock to you as it was to any of us."

"It was." Yet Claire knew that in the social scheme of things, she wasn't deserving of sympathy. She was only the neighbor, not one of the children, not one of the in-laws. Still, Ella Starnes had been like a mother to her.

"I knew, like you probably did, that she hadn't been feeling well lately, but…" He let the explanation drift.

"I saw her just the day before. Her color was fine, and she seemed better than she'd been all winter. She was even talking about taking a cruise this fall."

Hunter snorted, and shook his head, as if his mother's antics would never cease to amaze him. "Up until this last year, she sure knew how to enjoy life," he grudgingly admitted. "Beth said maybe it's a blessing, that she went quickly like that. She never would have stood for being sick, or being a burden day in and day out."

Claire nodded, momentarily thinking how strange it was that they could talk about anything at all, even his mother's death. "I know. If anything, your mother taught me how to fight back." He looked at her quickly, making Claire immediately wish she could retract the words. But she couldn't, so she amended them. "Your mother knew how to take things in stride. She was too feisty to let her arthritis get her down, and too strong willed to have anything but a smile on her face."

Hunter made a funny little noise in the back of his throat, as if he was choking up and couldn't risk saying anything.

Instinctively Claire knew he didn't want to cry, or look weak, in front of her. So she tried to make a joke—as feeble as it was—to give him an out. "Of course, she did have a thing about the driveway," she said. "She kept telling me that shoveling it was good exercise, that it would keep *me* young. She bought me a new shovel every fall. I, on the other hand, kept hinting about a *snowblower*...."

He laughed, hard enough to explain away the red-rimmed, watery eyes. He swiped at them with the back of his hand, as if it was her poor joke that had brought tears to his eyes.

But they both knew better.

Claire longed to give him a hug and tell him she was really, truly sorry. But rational thought warned her that would be a particularly bad idea, given how she felt about him.

So they stood there, grappling with a strained moment of silence. Claire realized she should make some kind of excuse and leave, but couldn't bring herself to do so. It had been years, what were a few more miserable minutes? Especially if she could share them with Hunter.

"So you caught me," he said finally, changing the subject as he shook out the T-shirt. "I was about to jump in the shower before the girls and their families got in." He pulled the shirt over his head, shouldering into the sleeves before yanking down the hem, and stretching it taut against his chest. Hunter's biceps moved as though he was a day laborer, not a pampered entrepreneur. Claire suspected he probably popped the seams out of his designer suits. "Left my car in the street, so that's why you probably didn't notice it. I figured they'd be unloading playpens and high chairs and stuff."

Regret unexpectedly went zinging through her middle, and she looked away, refusing to let him see the longing she couldn't control. She was slowly coming to terms with the fact that she'd probably never have a family, never have a child, but some days were more difficult than others.

When she and Hunter were eighteen, and full of hope for the future, they'd impulsively picked out baby names. She wondered if he still remembered. April Michelle for a girl. Tyler Worth for a boy. She'd once written them in all the margins of her spiral-bound notebooks and imagined the beautiful babies they'd have. Now all she had was empty, empty arms.

"My mistake," she said, forcing a calm into her voice that she didn't feel. "To tell you the truth, if I'd known you were here, Hunter, I certainly wouldn't have walked in. I would have stopped one of your sisters in the driveway and handed them the casserole."

Both of his eyebrows lifted, and he regarded her perceptively. "Still mad, huh?"

She stared at him, considered the blunt question, and reminded herself that maybe she was one lucky woman. She could have married him twelve years ago and been saddled with him for the duration. "Why would I be mad? We haven't talked in a dozen years. We don't have anything in common. You have your life in California, I've kept mine in Lost Falls. We clearly don't have anything to say to each other. You're just one more part of my past." She held up the key. "Look. Here's your mother's house key. I'm sure you'll want it back."

His eyes dropped, flicking over the brass key. "Keep it."

"There's no reason to keep it. Not now."

His gaze went hard, penetrating, the green flecks in his eyes fading to bronze. "Mom appreciated everything you did for her, Claire. You were here for her every day when none of the rest of us were. None of us will forget that. No matter what happened between you and me."

Claire chose to ignore the last sentence. "Your sisters came as often as they could. It was hard for them, living so far from home, and I was happy to fill in when I could. But, your mother, she's gone now…and…"

Claire tried not to strangle over the words. For herself, for Hunter, for even the awkwardness of the situation. Yet with Ella gone, Claire's ties to the Starnes family were forever severed.

The sudden, helpless feeling that she was all alone made her shiver with the strangest sense of claustrophobia. She wouldn't think about the anxiety that had been building in her all day, she wouldn't even consider it. There were worse things in life than being alone.

Finally, she said, "Experience tells me you'll want to pull in all the stray keys, Hunter. Or at least change the locks."

He still didn't reach for the key, and Claire, left holding it, stared at him.

"You're as good as family, Claire."

Claire's hand dropped slightly. She let the palm of her hand swallow the key and curled her fingers tightly around it. "Blood's thicker than water, we both know that."

A second slipped away. His gaze was pinned on her. There wasn't a hint of sexual suggestion behind his eyes, just a steady evaluation. "You look good, Claire. Really good."

How could he say something like that, she fumed. How? Why couldn't he just politely thank her for the blasted pot pie and show her the door?

Tension sizzled, and she insanely thought of the key Benjamin Franklin had threaded on the kite string to conduct a little electrical current. Right now, Hunter Starnes was like that, offering her one fantastic lightning bolt after another. "I also wanted to let you know," she said evenly, "if you need anything—"

"A truce?"

Claire's eyelids involuntarily went half-mast, and her heart fluttered. "Don't."

"C'mon, Claire. This is ridiculous," he growled, imperceptibly moving toward her. "We haven't even said hello. Not a real hello. You're standing on your side of the room, I'm standing on mine. We both know we aren't going to take up where we left off, but we can at least be civil."

"I think this is probably best. Before we let that other stuff cloud our vision."

He frowned, his eyebrows going into a straight, hard line. "Other stuff? What other stuff? What the hell are you talking about?"

She needed to tell him? Stuff like stolen kisses and intimate discoveries and necking out on Pine Lake Road. "Teenage hormones," she said succinctly. "Teenage encounters of the worst kind."

"Oh, Claire, come on! We were kids!"

"Exactly. I'm older and wiser now."

A heartbeat skipped away as his gaze flicked over her. "You're better."

She heard just enough of the husky approval in his voice to know he meant it, and that unnerved her. "Hunter, don't. Don't take me at face value. You don't know me at all. Not anymore."

He took a tentative step toward her. "What I do know is that in all these years, you never let my mother down." Claire steeled herself to dismiss his words, to dismiss him—but Hunter took another step in her direction. "I know she thought the world of you, Claire. I know I've never forgotten you, no matter how badly we parted."

Claire scrunched her eyes closed. She didn't want praise. She didn't want explanations. She'd only wanted to do the right thing by Ella, as hard as it had been, and as hard as Hunter had made it for her. "Hunter—"

Before she could reply, he looped his arms around her back and drew her full-length against his chest. "Hush. Just for a minute," he whispered against her ear. "Because there's a part of me that needs you now."

Ripples of longing, of empathy, coursed through her, and Claire struggled to repulse each and every one of them. It would have been so easy to sag against him, to absorb his heat, his strength, to let herself go…but she stoically refused to do it. "Hunter…" she said softly, gently pulling back and trying to extricate herself, "…don't."

Claire Dent, Hunter realized, was the epitome of strength. In his arms, she was as willowy as a sapling, as resilient as a rock. Her hair was longer now, at least four inches past her shoulders, in a wavy, loose style that was invitingly silky, sexy.

In high school she had curled and crimped her hair into submission. Now he wondered why she'd ever bothered.

He also wondered why the hell he'd never realized what she'd grow into.

She was a beauty. Simple as that. Everything about her was seductively simple. From her khaki slacks to the powder-blue T-shirt top she wore. Pearl studs in her ears and the sheerest of makeup. Her skin was flawless, and her high cheekbones carried a natural blush.

She didn't have the hollowed-out, starved look of a cover model; her face was firm and full, the curve of her jaw solid. Her nose was so straight and perfect that she could have posed as the scale model for a plastic surgeon.

But it was Claire's darker-than-mocha gaze that leveled a man. Her deep-set eyes were so luminous that he'd caught himself searching for a reflection in their depths. She'd always had a brooding, thoughtful quality shadowing her eyes, but then, that was no wonder, given what she'd been through.

"Hunter...don't," she repeated.

Claire's lower lip, which was provocatively fuller than the top, had always had the most incredible way of working around a word. It worked that way now. With that single word. *Don't.* He ought to heed the warning, but he couldn't help goading her. "Don't what?"

Claire pursed her lips and spat out the answer, "You know *what!*"

Inside, he ached to laugh. His mother used to claim Claire Dent didn't pout very often, but when she did it was the prettiest little pout this side of the Mississippi. He was inclined to agree.

Hunter slowly, reluctantly, released her.

She'd found herself. He could see it in every mannerism,

in the way she carried herself and the way she talked. She was a woman, confident and assured. She'd grown up—and he experienced a glimmer of regret that he hadn't been around to see it.

"I just needed a 'welcome back home.' And," he admitted, "maybe a little hug."

"I'm not the one to offer it, Hunter. We both know that."

"Claire, the first half of my life you were my best friend. I don't want to spend the last half of my life thinking I've made you my enemy."

"I'm not your enemy," she denied. "I doubt thoughts like that will keep you up at night. I just want to walk out of this awkward situation with some class, that's all."

"You want to go out of this with class?" he repeated. "Fine. I'll let you. But first, before you walk back out that door, let's resolve our hard feelings. I say we kiss and make up."

Chapter Two

Hunter's mouth brushed over hers. She should have stopped him, Claire thought dizzily, before she allowed his powerfully sweet kiss to addle her brain and destroy her defenses.

Yet Hunter didn't overpower her, and his mouth made no demands. Instead he expertly touched and tasted, meeting her hunger halfway. In a gesture of comfort that did seem to have some inexplicable healing power.

Years and burdens fell away as he magically carried her back to her youth, to memories that were steeped in expectation and hope. He lifted her, and she soared, weightless for the first time in years.

No hard feelings? she thought woozily. Everything about him was hard. The way he held her, the way he cradled her. The way his fingers pressed into her back, drawing her to him, the way his knee instinctively sluiced between her legs, taking possession.

It would have been easy to give herself up to the kiss. Remarkably easy. But she restrained herself, slapping a conscious rein on her emotions, willing her tongue to still, her lips to cease their explorations.

Hunter pulled away, the coarse stubble on his cheek grazing hers. "Now that," he whispered huskily, "makes me feel like I've come back home."

His arms dropped loosely to her sides, his fingertips sliding down the length of her forearms and her wrists. She imperceptibly drew back, shaking him off.

"Hunter," she said shakily, "that won't happen again. You can joke and say that we've kissed and made up. But all we will ever be toward each other is polite. Anything else is out of the question. We can be neighbors for the few days you're here. But anything more than that is—"

"Out of the question?"

She took a step back, regret nipping at her heels. "Yes. I think maybe we understand each other now."

"Don't count on it, Claire. I never did things the easy way. You, better than anyone, should know that."

"The whole town knows that, Hunter. Because you didn't just walk out on me, you walked out on your dad and your mom. They expected you to run the station, to keep it going."

"It wasn't what I wanted," he retorted, dismissing her reproach.

"Apparently, neither was I," she pointed out softly. She turned to go, then stopped at the back door, the key still in her hand. It was all she could do to walk away from him, but she forced herself to do it. "I meant to tell you. I know you'll be crowded here, and there's no good place to stay within thirty miles. So, if you decide you need an extra bedroom, someone's welcome to use the guest bedroom at my place. You can let them know."

She opened the door and had one foot on the steps.

"Thanks, Claire. I'll bring my stuff over later."

She swung around to face him, unable to wipe the surprise off her face. "You'll what?"

"I'll shower first, then bring my stuff over," he said nonchalantly, "after the girls get in."

"I didn't mean you," she stammered. "I meant Courtney or Lynda or—"

"You'll want me," he said decidedly.

Her eyes widened.

"That is, I'm the one that's the best houseguest. The girls and their families are loud and noisy and on a schedule that runs counterclockwise to the rest of the world."

"I can adjust." She'd have to adjust, because there was no way she could live in the same house with Hunter. Not even for a few days.

"But Courtney's baby is colicky. Beth's little boy has asthma and—"

"I know that."

"But he'd probably be allergic to your cat."

"What! How do you know I have a cat?" Claire bristled, incensed that he knew even one intimate detail about her. Huh. He probably regarded her as an old maid who had nothing to do except sit around carrying on conversations with her cat.

"Mom mentioned it. Said you found the kitten in her garage."

"Well, she couldn't take care of it," she said defensively. "That was the winter she went on that whale-watching cruise."

He chuckled. "Mmm, nice of you to take it in, though. Even so, it would most likely send Brendon into an asthma attack. Cat dander, and all that."

Claire grimaced. Okay. She didn't want to be responsible for *that*. "Then maybe Mindy. Or Lynda…"

"I don't know. Mindy's husband is a lovable guy, but an uncontrollable slob. And frankly, they bicker all the time. But you probably already know that, too. Lynda's better half works nights, and when he isn't working he's up banging around the kitchen, making omelettes and frying up hash browns." He lifted his broad shoulders. "Looks like you're stuck with me."

She stepped back inside the kitchen. "No. Not a good idea. It wouldn't look good for you to be in my house."

"Why not?"

She sputtered. "Because—because *someone* might think we were taking up where we left off."

"So?"

"So it matters to me what people think—and I don't want you in my home."

To his credit—or amazing acting abilities—Hunter recoiled, as if he'd been hurt. "I just thought it would be the best all-around solution," he said. "For both of us. Since you were willing to help us out, and I simply want to fly under the radar with my sisters' families."

"Hunter, we both know it goes way beyond that."

He gave her a long, assessing gaze, one that made Claire waffle. She needed to dismiss those tawny-colored eyes, that suggestive slant of his mouth. He wasn't going to talk her into this. He wasn't! But even as her mind was saying 'no,' her body was saying 'yes.' She could feel herself gravitating to him, as much as she wanted to deny it.

"I was only taking you up on your offer for a place to stay because I wanted a little peace and quiet. Just while the girls are here. Then I'll move out, I swear. Nobody even needs to know I'm there, if it embarrasses you."

Claire paused, her blood growing even hotter—and for an

entirely different reason. Hunter didn't know what embarrassment and humiliation was. But she'd faced it down. For twelve years after he'd left, she'd stared it in the eye and risen above it. If he thought he could just move in with her and resume their old comfortable relationship—

"Hey, I'll sneak in after dark and leave before dawn."

The implications sent a curling sensation through Claire's middle—making her feel as if he was intentionally taking that impulsive kiss one step further. "Now that would be an even worse idea."

"Look, Claire," he reasoned, "we're going to have to get past this. I'm going to be here for a while to settle Mom's estate. We're going to be neighbors for a few weeks, like it or not. But as soon as the girls leave to go home and get all their kids back in school and their activities, my energies go to putting this place in order. I don't even have time to make nice with you. I want to get the job done and get out of here."

Claire should have been hurt. But she wasn't. In fact, it was almost a relief to know where he stood and what he intended to do. In the meantime, she'd bash back her inclinations and brace up her defenses. She'd drive him out of her mind and banish him from her soul. She would *not* let him get the best of her.

For she knew, without another word between them, that in the next few hours she'd relent and Hunter would move into her home as a houseguest. But she'd absolutely, positively draw the line at letting him move back into her heart.

Hunter moved in with a matched set of leather luggage, and an apologetic smile. He stood uncomfortably in the kitchen of the frame home she'd inherited from her mother and eyed the new wallpaper with the whimsical birdhouse border. His gaze flitted over the remodeled kitchen. The oak cabinets were a far cry from the dark avocado-green ones he probably remembered. The refinished claw-foot table now had four matching chairs, instead of five spindly castoffs. "I didn't mean to strong-arm you over this, Claire."

"Sure you did," she said easily, putting the coffee carafe back on the burner. At the same time, she wondered whether he was having second thoughts. "The coffee's all set for tomorrow morning. If you get up before me, all you have to do is turn it on."

"Thanks."

"Help yourself to whatever you need," she said breezily, wishing the moment she uttered the words she could take them back. What could the man possibly need? Intimate confessions at midnight? Another stolen kiss behind closed blinds? A little pleasure in the pantry? "Bread's in the bread box," she said, "eggs in the fridge and cereal's on the top shelf over the stove. I don't do much more than yogurt for breakfast—and I eat that in the car." She paused. "I'll be out early tomorrow, Hunter. I've got a house to show. So I've left a key on the table. I'll be in and out, so our paths probably won't even cross. Don't worry about that."

He looked. The key ring, an advertising piece for Falls Company Real Estate, offered a single brass key. "Sounds like you're trying to avoid me."

"No. I've got a house to sell and a living to make, that's all."

He nodded slowly. "Funny to think of you as a real estate agent now. I remember the time you had to beg Mrs. Montgomery for the receptionist's job. So? You like it?"

"It was probably the single best thing that ever happened to me." Polite conversation, she reminded herself, that was the *only* thing they needed to make together. Yet the phrases *make time, make music, make love* went zinging through her head.

He nodded again, his attention fixed on the pot rack over the work island.

"With a kitchen like this I know you've learned how to cook."

"Enough to get by. But I don't like to eat alone." Hunter shifted his big, muscular frame, nailed her with a look, then let the implication slide. They should have been husband and wife by now, she thought miserably. She should have been making him eggs and kissing him out the door in the morning. They should have had sleeper-clad feet padding to their bedside before dawn.

"You've changed things around here so much, Claire, I wouldn't have recognized the place."

"Things don't stay the same, Hunter. Of course, people don't stay the same, either. But I guess you've figured that out."

He snorted, inclining his head slightly. "I would have recognized you, though."

"Really?"

"Mmm. I could have been a block away, on Main Street, and picked you out of a crowd." She waited, feeling her eyelashes drop a coquettish fraction of an inch, wondering what he meant. "You've got this tilt in your get-along. It's the way you walk."

"A tilt in my get-along?" Claire repeated, acutely conscious that Hunter's comment was slightly suggestive.

He chuckled. "And the way you twist yourself around. You have this distinctive way you lean back from the hip and look over your shoulder. You did it on the back-porch steps today. Just like I remembered."

"I think the explanation for that is startled. I was *startled* that you'd think my invitation included you." She grabbed a tea towel off the counter, folded it and hung it over the oven door. "I certainly never saw that coming."

"Hey. I always did like to keep you guessing, Claire."

"No guessing games this time around, Hunter," she warned. She wouldn't be able to bear it if he started teasing her again, not like the old times. He wouldn't, of course. Because his eyes were shadowed, and his grief was palpable. No, his mind was on another kind of loss.

"Well—" he lifted a shoulder "—I appreciate you putting me up anyway. Being around the girls and their families makes me feel like an outsider. Like I'm the odd man out, the one who's in the way."

"Hunter, your sisters wouldn't make anyone feel like an outsider. And I doubt you're in the way."

"Mmm, no," he said dryly, "not when it comes to lifting and carrying." He leaned against the countertop. "They already put me to work. I hauled in two high chairs, a bunch of diaper bags, a playpen, and then, before I came over, I put a portable crib together."

Claire's gaze drifted to the empty spot against the far wall. She'd intentionally saved that space for a high chair. It didn't look as if that was going to happen. "At least you made yourself useful," she said coolly.

"The girls wondered when you were coming over."

"I thought about it. But I wanted to give them some time alone. It's always hard, going into the house for the first time, realizing the people you love aren't there anymore."

He thoughtfully flicked the zipper tab on the shaving kit tucked under his arm. It was a muscular gesture, one that put a curling sensation through Claire's middle. "They appreciated the hot meal, Claire. Said it was just like you, to do something like that."

Claire ignored the praise. She couldn't bear it if he was nice to her; she'd rather be dismissed. She'd learned how to deal with that.

"They also said you should be there with us, eating."

A lump formed in Claire's throat as she imagined taking her place at the Starnes family dinner table. She once thought that those girls would be her sisters-in-law, that she would be part of the family. "How's everybody holding up?"

He looked away, considering. "Lynda's family is staying with friends, so I haven't seen much of her. But Courtney's pretty upset," he admitted. "She was planning a trip back next month, and she feels guilty, like she should have arranged her trip sooner, to get here before…well, you know."

Claire nodded. Courtney was the sensitive one. The one who nursed the sickliest-looking plants back to health. The one who chased flies out of the house rather than pick up a flyswatter. "The last thing your mother would have tolerated was Courtney's guilt. You find a way to tell her that."

Hunter offered her a searching gaze; one Claire was totally unprepared for. She remembered the last time he'd looked at her like that—when he'd told her he was moving out of town, and he'd wanted her to say it was okay.

"You always had a way of making people feel better, didn't you? I remember you offered up a few suggestions I listened to."

"No. Not always," she said, avoiding the magnetic color of his irises. "I can think of one in particular you didn't listen to."

Once more, the reminder of their broken love affair skittered through the room.

"I wasn't ready, Claire," he said finally. "It wouldn't have worked. Not back then. Not for either of us."

Claire pinned him with a look. "Don't tell me something I already know, Hunter. I would have been miserable with you, and we both know it." Hunter's eyes narrowed; obviously that was not the answer he expected. Not from her. She had loved him so desperately, he'd believed she'd always wait for him. But the waiting game had long been over. She didn't want to talk about it, either, not with a man who still turned her inside out with a want she couldn't control. "Come on, let me show you to your room," she invited, heading into the hall. "It's a little fluffy for you, but I'm sure you'll get along."

"Fluffy?" he inquired, tossing his garment bag over his arm and dragging his suitcase along behind him. "That sounds like something you'd name a cat, not do to a room."

Claire smiled, in spite of her resolve not to. "No, the cat's name is Zoey, and she has very little patience for anyone who does not come bearing tuna." She paused at the foot of the stairs, in the front foyer.

"I'll keep that in mind," he said, noting that the newel post, banister and balusters had been replaced with turned oak. The bare lightbulb was gone, replaced by an oak and glass fixture. Everything was warmer, more inviting. Without all the laundry piled on the stairs, or the space by the front door clogged with worn-out tennis shoes and book bags and jackets, the foyer looked ten times bigger than he remembered—and, for once, it looked *loved*.

Claire started up the wide staircase, now carpeted in a rich, oyster-colored hue.

"I made my room over into a guest room and took Momma's room. Because it was bigger and in the front of the house," Claire said.

Hunter hesitated, momentarily unnerved to think he'd sleep in Claire's old room, the one she'd had as a teenager. He hadn't expected that. He'd only wanted to be in the house with her, alone, to reinforce, in his own mind, that he'd made the right decision all those years ago. Yet he was already questioning it. Why, that single kiss had only served to remind him that there was such a thing as cataclysmic chemistry.

"It's probably a whole lot less than what you're used to," she went on, pausing at the top of the steps, "but it's the best I've got."

"It'll be fine," he answered, moving up the last two steps and toward the open door of her room. It took him three steps to cross the hall, and then he stopped short on the threshold, wondering at the time warp that had fashioned the differences in their lives. He remembered a broken-down twin bed, cheap, torn shades on the windows, and walls with a few odd posters and tons of pictures torn from her mother's magazines. "Huh." His shoulders slumped, taking it all in. "Looks a little different without the posters."

"That was a kid thing, a stage. Now I call this the 'garden room.'"

"My." The rough plaster-and-lath walls were painted eggshell, a mere backdrop for blue and salmon colors. Gauzy white curtains hung behind the plaid tab-top drapes and complimented the floral and checked bedding. It was a remarkable makeover, of bold strength and delicate fragility. He walked into the room and put his suitcase at the end of the bed. "You are either a chameleon or an escape artist, to change a room like this."

She laughed behind him, as if she found something about his statement genuinely funny. "I'm not the escape artist. You are. I stayed *here* to make something of myself."

He rolled the implication over in his head. She was hurt, and by golly, she was going to take every opportunity to remind him that he was responsible for it. "That was a poor choice of words, wasn't it?"

"Yes. I'd say so." She tipped her head and walked into the

room. "Okay. There's plenty of hangers in the closet, and I cleaned out a drawer for you. Extra blankets and towels on the top shelf of the closet. No phone, no TV, no amenities."

He tossed his garment bag on the bed, atop the sprigged duvet, and ran a hand over the foot of the iron bed. "Nice and quiet, though."

"Mmm, we do have plenty of that around Lost Falls."

There were fresh flowers on the table, but Hunter quickly realized she hadn't brought them in for his benefit. It was Claire, filling up her life and redoing all the things that had been absent when she was growing up. She paused to smooth a crease from the pillow slip and Hunter watched, mesmerized by the gentle, feminine gesture.

"Recognize it?" she asked.

"Excuse me?"

"The bed," she prompted.

He looked down, frowning. It was an old-fashioned double bed, the iron frame painted ochre, the headboard high and round, the footboard like a cameo on its side.

"Your mother gave it to me," she went on. "From the cabin."

His jaw slid off center. "No? That old bed frame we had in the barn? We propped it against the door one summer, to keep the dog in."

"I found all the parts and pieces, and she was cleaning out and wanted to get rid of it…."

His hand trailed over the joints of the iron rungs. "Beautiful. What you've done to it, Claire."

"I was glad to have it. Kind of like a hand-me-down, to remind me of the cabin."

He snorted, smiling on the inside as the distant memories crowded into his mind. "We had a lot of fun out there, didn't we?"

"It was my favorite place ever," she said. He watched her doe-dark eyes go soft, and reluctantly admitted there wasn't a woman on the face of the earth to compare to Claire. "I felt like a new person every time I was out there. Of course, there was that one time…"

He turned, intentionally arching an eyebrow at her. "Only *one* time?" he asked. "We had the craziest things happen to us out there. Remember the time you said 'move over' and I fell out of the hayloft?" He shook his head. "I wore that cast for six weeks. And it was the middle of summer. Wrecked my whole baseball season."

"So? It wasn't my fault. What about the time we played cops and robbers and you tied me up and *left* me there? Out in the woods."

"I was coming back."

"Yeah. Right. If Beth hadn't come along, I'd probably still be there."

He couldn't stop the slow, amused smile that eased across his face. "You were spittin' mad. Had to bribe you with a quarter candy bar just to get you to talk to me again." He laughed, remembering how much it had meant to him to earn his way back into Claire's good graces. "And then there was that treasure hunt you concocted to find the gold at the end of the rainbow."

"Me? You were the one who wanted the gold."

"Well, you were the one who dug it out of your mother's purse and gave it to me."

Claire rolled her eyes, remembering. "Oh, I got in so much trouble. In my whole life I've never gotten in so much trouble as I did that one time, for losing that ring."

"We didn't lose it," he reminded, "we buried it. My folks turned that place upside down looking for it."

"Back then I had no idea what it meant to my mom. Or else I wouldn't have done anything so stupid." She paused. "A month's worth of rent and a summer's worth of groceries."

Hunter rapped the iron bed frame with the back of his knuckles, pensively remembering all they had once shared. Even with all the struggles, it had been an idyllic childhood, very much removed from the real world.

"It was a world away," he allowed, marveling that for moments they could reminisce and talk and laugh as they once did. "I've thought about the place a few times since I've left. But it's the strangest thing... I don't miss it. I wanted to leave so badly that I don't think I've missed anything at all about Lost Falls." His head swiveled, as he realized what he'd said, expecting her to be angry. "Except you."

Chapter Three

As astonishment rolled through Claire's eyes, all he could recognize was his blunder. "I meant," he revised quickly, "that I've missed having you as a friend."

"We haven't been friends for a long time, Hunter," Claire reminded him. "You went your way, I went mine."

"You didn't go anywhere, Claire. Like you said, you stayed here."

"And was that so bad?"

"Maybe not. Not for you. You worked your way up in the company."

She stared at him in disbelief. "My life here is more than working my way up in a real estate office, Hunter," she said evenly. "My life is not just about a *job*. It's about commitments, and a sense of community and belonging."

"Funny. I seem to remember a time when you didn't feel that way at all. I remember when you talked about seeing the world, when you talked about shedding the old memories and trading them in on some new ones. Ones that you'd created—not the ones that you were saddled with."

Claire winced. Hunter's reminders of the rough times her family had endured hurt. "I'd rather you didn't bring that up," she said, her eyes flashing. "My father—"

"I'm not talking about him," he said. "This is about you, Claire. You always held your head up, no matter what happened. You never had anything to be ashamed of, and you made sure people knew it. But by staying here, you have a bundle of baggage attached to your backside."

"That was a long time ago, Hunter," Claire reminded. "And I let go of it a long time ago."

He paused, his gaze narrowing, his expression thoughtful. "Why, then," he asked, "can't you do the same with us?"

The unexpected question stopped Claire cold. Apprehension gripped her middle, making her heart pound and putting an ugly pain behind her breastbone. "You misunderstand," she said finally, carefully. "There hasn't been an 'us' for a long, long time."

"But you still can't let go of it."

"Because…" She pressed her lips firmly together, and let the moment of weakness and indecision pass. She couldn't allow herself to tell him he had been her everything, that he'd been her world, her life, her passion. Instead she settled for, "You were different. That's why. I trusted you." She stepped away, to the dresser, and picked up the faded family photo that she'd framed. Skimming her thumb over the top of the frame, she wiped away any trace of dust, then handed it to him. "I remember the day this picture was taken."

He studied it, his expression quizzical. Her father wasn't even looking at the camera, and her mother was frowning, her mouth clamped tight. It looked as if they'd been arguing.

"But…you couldn't have been much more than seven or eight."

"Even so, I remember it. Because you were standing behind the lilac bushes watching." He looked up at her in surprise. "You were waiting to see if I could go play. And that's how I remember you, always on the perimeter. Always there. Always waiting for me, no matter what. And because of that I gave you everything."

A trace of annoyance touched his forehead, then he slowly, carefully, slid the picture back on the dresser. "We were next-door neighbors, Claire. We grew up together."

"But I grew up giving you my hopes and dreams. You knew me better than I knew myself. And sometimes I could just look at you and know what you were thinking." Her voice dropped to a painful whisper. "Hunter, you were my first—"

His palm lifted and his fingers splayed to prevent her from uttering "lover." "I didn't take *that* intimacy," he emphasized, "lightly. I still don't. But we were eighteen years old, Claire. Back then," he admitted, "I was naive enough to think we would be together forever."

"We could have been," she countered, painfully aware of his masculine good looks, his deep rich voice. "But of course the ink had to go and dry on your college diploma."

He let a second slip away, his gaze expressionless. "You could have come with me."

"I had responsibilities," she argued. "I couldn't just leave."

"I asked you to postpone the wedding and come with me."

"You remember things a little differently than I do," she said, nailing him with a look that spoke volumes. "Because I don't remember being asked, I remember being told."

"I wasn't going to turn down that job!"

"So you turned me down instead."

"Don't say it like that!" He raked a hand over the top of his head. "I didn't turn you down, and I didn't turn away from you." Claire watched as the muscles in his jaw thumped and his mouth went thin, hard. "I needed to move on. I couldn't bear the thought of spending the rest of my life in that station, pumping gas, giving directions and filling the paper-towel dispenser every morning. I thought, ultimately, I'd be doing the right thing by you. That we'd both be better off."

"Well, maybe you did do the right thing," she said. "Because when you left I found out how strong I was." She purposely gave herself a moment to pull herself together, to say the one thing she needed to say. "I found out that I could stop loving you."

Hurt flickered in the depths of his gold-flecked eyes. "Claire…"

She shook her head, remembering him in his youth. She refused to submit to the feelings coursing through her as he stood before her now—a man determined and confident, one who thrived in his single, solitary life. "No. Don't say anything, because that's exactly how I feel. Maybe you did do me a favor by leaving. Tonight's the first night of the second part of our life, and we both need to know where we stand and how far we'll go toward trusting one another. We had a past…but now we're just two people sharing the same house. That's all. Two people thrown together by necessity does not create much of a future, and certainly not a friendship. You invited yourself, and I let you."

"I do appreciate you putting me up, Claire," he said stiffly.

She paused, momentarily looking away. "And Hunter? I'm genuinely sorry about your mother," she said, her voice filling with honest, heartfelt compassion. "But I'm equally sorry that it took your mother's loss for me to be able to talk to you again. Aside from this situation being awkward and uncomfortable, we both know it's temporary. Because we're both going in different directions after this."

Claire went back to her room with all the dignity she could muster. She grabbed her new pink nightgown out of the closet, mostly to remind herself that she was still feminine, still desirable and—unfortunately—still available. Then she crawled between the sheets of her bed, rolled over, put her face in her pillow and wept. She was mortified and angry and outraged. Mostly with herself—and a little bit with Hunter.

She couldn't believe she'd spoken to him like that. She couldn't believe that after all these years the yearning for him was still there, just below the surface. She didn't know what she'd wanted, but it wasn't any of what she'd gotten. Maybe she'd intended to prove to him that she was over him, that she was independent and confident.

Instead she'd laid the ground rules for a war, one that neither of them wanted and neither of them would win.

As if she hadn't suffered enough already, she had to compound her problems by telling him how she felt. About him. About her regrets. About what the intervening years had done to her, and how they'd changed her.

But he was here! In her house. And to add insult to injury, he was sleeping in the bedroom she'd grown up in. In the bed that she'd painstakingly refurbished. In the same spot where she'd lain awake at night and dreamed of all the things they could be, have and do together.

Ten years ago, she'd meticulously shaved that particular room of memories and memorabilia. She'd intentionally wiped away every last trace of Hunter Starnes. And now he was back, putting his individual fingerprints on everything new. She'd never again walk into that room without seeing him there. Without seeing his quizzical expression as she laid out the ultimatums. Or seeing his garment bag draped over the end of the bed. Or the way his gaze appreciatively drifted over to the fresh flowers on the bedside table.

It was more than unnerving. It was going to be her undoing.

Claire sniffed, then impatiently wiped her hot cheeks and wet eyes with the back of her hand and rolled over to stare up at the ceiling. Zoey jumped up on the bed, purring with empathy as she nudged her way under Claire's arm. She absently stroked the cat, her hand rhythmically sliding down Zoey's soft fur as she thought about Hunter. Zoey purred louder. The sound, and the repetitive motion, had a calming effect on Claire and her heart began to let go of a little of the pain.

It was unbelievable that she and Hunter were sharing the same house. She vaguely wondered what Ella would think. For a few moments, she imagined the conversation she'd have with Ella, who would have been brusque and no-nonsense.

Do what you have to do, so you have no regrets. You've got a lot of history together, Claire, no sense making a mess of what's left of it.

Why, she could even hear Ella admonishing her to be rational, be responsible and be herself.

It surprised her, how clearly she could hear Ella talking to her, especially about this. Initially, when Claire was raw and hurting from the breakup, Ella had given her advice and encouragement. But as the months passed, Ella skillfully avoided much mention of Hunter. When it was clear that he wasn't coming back, his name seemed to fade from Ella's vocabulary entirely. They talked, but their talk centered around their gardens, the weather, Claire's work at the real estate company, the women's group at church or Ella's latest trips.

They talked about the girls and their families, but never, ever Hunter.

Ella had laid the parameters, and Claire understood that the subject was off-limits. For years, they'd both accommodated the unspoken agreement. Yet Ella knew Claire had never completely gotten Hunter out of her system. It was something that didn't have to be talked about. Ella just knew.

Now Ella was gone…and Claire had no one to talk to at all. Not about the weather. Not about her newest listing. Not about how goofy it was to only serve regular coffee at church and not decaf. She'd never again have the opportunity to even avoid mentioning Hunter.

Yet Hunter was there, in her old room, just beyond the wall—and he was tormenting her imagination, just as he'd always done.

It was all so convoluted, really. He was a part of Ella and she was a part of him—and now Claire had to find a way to face life without either of them.

To lose Ella so unexpectedly had shaken her. To have Hunter return and be so physically close—and so emotionally distant—had deeper, more painful implications.

She swallowed convulsively, and a dull ache settled into her heart for all that should have been. For all they should have been to each other.

They should be sharing the same bed. They should have their heads on the same pillow, and they should be holding each other. She should be comforting him over the loss of his mother, and he should be finding solace in her arms. She should be able to tell him that it was his mother, not hers, who had been her strength and inspiration.

But they were separated by years and walls. The concrete

walls of plaster and wood; the abstract walls of miscommunication, denial and regret.

She squeezed her eyelids shut, and tucked Zoey into the crook of her arm. She imagined Ella's son beyond the wall, in her old room, his muscular body claiming the full-size bed, his head on the feather pillow. Tomorrow his aftershave would linger on the pillow slip, and the musky, manly scent of him would permeate the sheets.

He had changed so much. Changes had crept into every aspect of his demeanor, of his being. The way he held his car keys was something new. His fingers possessively curled around the golf insignia. Growing up he was always losing his keys, either throwing them casually aside or putting them through the wash in the pockets of his jeans. She had the feeling he no longer did that. And the insignia especially intrigued her, making her wonder if he actually did play golf, or merely hung out at some fancy club, schmoozing and making deals. In Lost Falls, he'd never once held a golf club. She distinctly remembered him saying he didn't see much point in chasing some little white ball all over creation; he'd thought the game looked boring and tedious. Apparently he'd changed his mind.

He also carried a money clip now, in the front pocket of his jeans instead of a billfold tucked into the back patch pocket. She'd seen him nonchalantly fish it out with the car keys, a clip fat with bills and plated in gold. She remembered the days when his billfold was empty and they'd pooled their quarters for milk shakes and hamburgers.

Physically, his body was rock solid, his shoulders more square. Deeply carved smile lines creased his mouth, while delicately etched ones fanned out from the corners of his eyes. Even the texture of his skin had changed. His cheeks were weathered, the flesh across his forehead thinner, finer. He was, simply put, older.

She regretted the fact, even as she marveled at how much sexier he'd become. Still there was no denying time had passed them by. He'd gone on with his life and she'd gone on with hers. Days had passed, one into another, and the dreams they'd once shared had slowly evaporated into misty, melancholy memories.

Next fall she'd be thirty-five. It was almost incomprehensible to think of it. She felt young on the inside, but six months ago her doctor warned her time was running out. Her body was changing and she'd found herself confronting the late-in-life, increased-risk phase for pregnancy. As if it mattered. There wasn't a man on the horizon, certainly not one who was willing to be called "daddy."

But, oh, how vivid her dreams were. She'd grown up longing for fat-cheeked, cherubic babies to nurture, a home to cherish and a husband to love. Now it didn't look as though that was ever going to happen. But she'd once thought she'd have it all—with Hunter. She'd foolishly believed they were destined to be together, that fate had intertwined their lives. Why, twenty years ago she couldn't imagine one facet of her life without him in it.

Then again, she'd survived twelve miserable years without him. She guessed—grudgingly—that she could tolerate having him back for one night. Or even a few days. Yet she had the strangest niggling thought that allowing Hunter to spend as much as one night in her home would ruin her best-laid plans to forget him. But he was here, and she couldn't prevent the memories from surging in his wake.

The way he strode into her house, head bent, shoulders hunched. The dazzling glint of his smile, one that was big enough for a toothpaste commercial, tempting enough for a kiss. The unique and intoxicating scent that trailed behind him, enveloping her in new car leather and a signature cologne. The possessive hand he placed on the small of her back. His voice. So silky with persuasion, so husky with grief.

Memories that she'd have to deal with, forget or ignore. Or, possibly, recover from.

She couldn't allow the memories to overwhelm her. She couldn't.

She didn't have time to dally with Hunter. She couldn't allow him to impose on her thoughts and sidetrack her intentions for a home and a family.

Her biological clock was ticking. And maybe Hunter couldn't hear it, but she could. Time was running out, and she wasn't wasting one more precious minute thinking about the man who had walked away from her and from the plans they'd once made. She was through with him, and she was over him, and no one or nothing could make her turn to him again. Not ever. Not if she put her foot down and refused to do it.

Yet, when she finally fell asleep, in the wee hours of the morning, it was Hunter's visage that haunted her dreams. It was Hunter who beckoned, and taunted and teased. And even in her dreams, Claire could feel the tension drain from her body—and all resistance and regrets were forgotten as she moved toward Hunter's outstretched arms.

Hunter was up. Claire was so surprised he was dressed and in the kitchen, she stopped short in the doorway and momentarily studied him.

He slumped in the chair at the kitchen table, a cup of coffee at his elbow, the Laramie newspaper spread in front of him. He wore a faded T-shirt, one that was a little too tight and hugged his wide shoulders and biceps. Beneath the table, mesh shorts sagged over his bent muscular legs. Seeing the coarse, curling hair on his legs put a knot in Claire's middle.

For a moment, she idly watched his bare feet slide over the new tile floor. His big toe flexed back and forth as he read.

His hair was mussed—endearingly mussed—and the stubble on his cheeks was dark and thick.

He looked so at home her heart clenched.

This was a domestic scene. It was picture-perfect, save for the fact that their relationship was as far from domestic as it could get.

"You're up early," she observed, coming into the room.

"Oh. Hi." The smile he offered her was engaging. "Couldn't sleep."

She nodded, suddenly unable to look at him and feeling guilty when another glimmer of attraction rolled through her, especially when she knew what he was really here for and why he couldn't sleep. She remembered what it was like when she'd lost her mother. An all-pervasive sadness, one she couldn't quite define or reconcile, had enveloped her. She hadn't been able to sleep or think straight for days. "Mmm. I suppose you have a lot to do today."

He nodded. "That's why I went for an early-morning run. To clear my head and organize my thoughts."

She moved to the refrigerator, then stopped short. Zoey stood on the throw rug, contentedly licking her paws, an opened can of tuna at her feet.

"I wanted to win over the cat, so I stopped at the convenience store for some gourmet tuna stuff."

"You wanted to win over the cat," she repeated. "My. Gourmet, too," she said. "Well, she won't be fit to live with." *Traitor,* Claire condemned, grimacing at Zoey, as she stepped around the self-satisfied feline and her extravagant meal. Claire pulled a carton of orange juice out of the fridge and poured herself a glass. "And you run now."

He shrugged. "Everybody runs now. It's the thing."

"I don't," she said flatly. She immediately regretted using that tone, but something about his generalization got under her skin, making her think of how, when he'd run before, he'd run out on all their plans and their life together. "Guess I'm not like everybody," she said lamely, trying to cover up the strained silence.

A moment passed, then two. Finally, Claire screwed up her courage and looked in his direction. His hazel eyes were assessing, and they flicked over her.

"Nope. Guess not," he conceded finally, his voice dropping to an oddly husky pitch. "You're most certainly not like everybody else."

"I only meant—"

"Don't explain, Claire."

The air hummed with tension, everything going electric, the room throbbing with a substance, a vibrancy she could discern. Awareness skittered between them and suddenly Claire didn't know where to look. Not at him, not out the window, not at Zoey, or the floor, or her shoes. So she concentrated on the orange juice and silently wished it was a good stiff drink, something that would fortify her senses—or dull them.

He lifted off the back of the chair, bringing himself to an upright position. "Claire?"

"Yes?" Her voice sounded faint, even to herself.

"I had a hard time being in your old room last night. Kept thinking of all the things we did together, all the things we enjoyed. I kept looking for signs that the old you was still there, in that room, and I couldn't find what I was looking for. Not anywhere. Not even in that picture."

"If you're looking for mementos, Hunter, they're a long time gone. I outgrew that part of my life. Just like you did."

"Still…"

"You didn't expect me to stay the same, did you?" she asked softly.

"I don't know, Claire. I don't know what I expected."

"It isn't any easier for me having you here, Hunter. I'm not sure I even want to share anything about my life with you. And having it happen, under these circumstances, makes it even worse." She hesitated. "You know that, don't you?"

"Do you really want to know what I think?"

"Yes."

He inclined his head slightly, pushed back from the table and levered himself out of the chair. He sauntered over to her. A good half head taller, he looked down at her, capturing her with his golden gaze. Awareness crackled between them, making Claire shift slightly away.

"Last night, I wouldn't have wanted to be anywhere else," he said, his voice low, controlled. "No matter how much we're both hurting. And even though it's all so tangled up together—from losing my mom to losing you and what we had between us—I'd still want to be here. With you."

Her heart twisted, and it was all she could do to force herself to look back at him. "But you wanted out," she said, her voice barely above a whisper.

"But that doesn't mean I didn't care. That I didn't think about you a thousand times since I left. When I drove into town yesterday, my first inclination was to walk through your back door instead of mine."

She wondered. How could a man who hadn't contacted a woman for years suddenly make a declaration about how many times he'd thought of her? Or even think about walking in, as if he'd never left?

"But you have to understand I still don't regret leaving, Claire," he stated bluntly. "And I never will. Because I knew we could never be happy, not until I'd tried to do what I'd set out to. And I agree, the thing I hate is that now when I have come back, we've got another kind of pain to deal with. Life is too damn short for any nice, polite courtesy. For the awkward moments. Or even the hard feelings."

Claire bit her bottom lip. "We were both young and dumb—and friendship, even the kind we had, fades. I understand that."

"I don't think it fades, Claire," he said softly, "I just think it changes."

Chapter Four

Hunter watched Claire go out the door and experienced a vague sense of chagrin. As if he shouldn't be letting her go, not alone, not even to work, not with all this hanging over their heads. There were distinct moments when he felt as if he should be protecting her, not provoking her with his presence, or even with the truth.

Yesterday he'd foolishly thought he could pull this off. He'd intended to win her over, get her to see that their separation had really been the best thing. That they'd made the right decision all those years ago, and she was being silly, childish even, to cling to the hopes and dreams they'd outgrown.

Unfortunately, Claire Dent was anything but childish…and Hunter was slowly, painfully, becoming aware of it. She was confident, determined and motivated. She'd grown into herself. Not only was she a looker, but she also held center stage in the outlook department.

If he'd been out in California he wouldn't have thought

twice about whisking her away for some quality time. He'd have just done it. Nothing would have stopped him from getting to know her, from stripping away the layers of her façade—from the hurt to the vulnerability—and discovering every intimate inch of her.

But this was Claire. In Lost Falls, Wyoming. Things moved at a different pace out here.

Of course, even if the pace was different, men were the same. That part gnawed at him. He wondered, curiously, how many men had come between him and the twelve years they'd spent apart.

A twinge of jealousy churned through his middle. He hadn't been exactly celibate in the last twelve years. But Claire?

He wondered.

He wondered how many men had seen her smile grow and spread and mature. That secret smile that Hunter had once thought was the next best thing to a teaser in a girlie magazine. Of course, that was when he was a kid.

Yesterday, when he saw the beginnings of a smile hover on her mouth, he'd had some pretty provocative thoughts. It was one of the reasons he'd pushed her with that "kiss and make up" line. He'd had to taste her, touch her, if only to prove to himself that she could no longer torture him with a kiss, a touch.

But some things never change.

Taking a deep cleansing breath, he pushed the memory of their kiss out of his mind and glanced around the room, taking mental note of how many other things in her life had changed. Her father's beer bottles no longer overflowed the trash bin. Her mother's movie magazines no longer cluttered the dining room table. Paint no longer peeled off the windowsills because new vinyl ones had replaced them. The glass wasn't cloudy and smudged. It sparkled, and a sun catcher—one fashioned in a whimsical design with a sun and birds and flowers and a rainbow—hung from a gold cord.

To make it even more interesting, Claire now had the pet she'd always wanted. A fluffy gray cat who poised on the windowsill and occasionally batted at the sun catcher.

Everywhere he looked he saw Claire's little touches, her individual flair and her distinctive choices. A collection of birdhouses on the far wall. Tea towels embroidered with robins and sunflowers. A bird's nest on a tiny shelf above the bathroom door, next to the weathered metal sign from Carleton's Drug Store.

Claire had given strict attention to detail. So much so that it bothered him. She'd obviously invested heavily into her life, intending to make everything around her picture-perfect. Yet something was missing. Hunter couldn't put his finger on it, but he could feel it.

He wondered how things would have looked if he'd stayed. Would he have felt at home in this kitchen? With her as his wife? Would she have made a concerted effort to keep their life orderly? Would she have asked his opinion about putting up the wallpaper border of the birds and the bees? Or would she just have done it? For a moment he imagined Claire balancing on a step stool, in her jeans and up to her elbows in wallpaper paste, and he regretted that he hadn't been here to see that fiasco.

Then, without warning, the lyrics from a popular old tune went zinging through his head, about the birds and the bees.

Yes, he silently brooded, he knew all about the birds and the bees. With Claire. Thanks to Claire and because of Claire. She was the most passionate woman he'd ever had the privilege to know. Of course, he hadn't realized it back then. Not when he was pushing twenty. She'd possessed kisses that were sweeter than honey. She knew how to pleasure a man, to make everything drift into a hazy, mind-dulling kind of craving.

It was odd, the intoxicating effect she'd had on him.

For after twelve years of being away, of building his career and making a name for himself, he'd been in contact with a broad range of women. Women who knew how to drive a hard bargain. Prosperous, affluent women. Women who were raised on culture and educated on the continent. Women who could talk contracts in the morning, put together deals in the afternoon and seal them over a pricey glass of wine at night. Women who had scandalous affairs and laughed about it. Women who were sexy, and seductive and smart. Women who had it all.

Yet none of them had held a candle to Claire.

Strange, no matter what was thrown at that girl, she handled it with class. She could tip back a glass of tap water and make it look like the most exotic thing since an umbrella-clad strawberry margarita. She could be given a job, and if she didn't know anything about it, she'd find a way to get it done and get it done right. She could talk to anyone and make an impression. The right impression, the one that earned trust and respect and admiration.

Maybe those were the reasons why, when she issued the last ultimatum about the wedding, the one that sounded particularly like "now or never," he went ahead and walked, secure in the knowledge she'd be okay. He'd seen her pull herself up by her bootstraps dozens of times and she'd always walked out of it like a lady, a classy lady who deserved the world and all its contents.

He hadn't wanted to end their relationship, but at the time, he was a kid and he hadn't seen any other way out. As the only boy in a family of girls, it was clear he was expected to take over the gas station and garage. But his aspirations were bigger than 40-weight oil and premium versus unleaded. Bigger than filling the pop machine and making sure there was solution in the buckets for cleaning windshields. His father had made a good, honest living, and there was nothing wrong with it. But Hunter had seen firsthand how hard his mom and dad worked, and he'd promised himself he wasn't ever going to do the same thing. He grew up understanding the slim profit margin on a gallon of gas. He'd spent his teen years watching his dad grumble about the weather with the old-timers or take the tow truck out in subzero temperatures to pull some idiot's car out of a ditch.

It wasn't what Hunter had wanted. Plain and simple as that. He'd wanted more, and he couldn't get what he'd wanted in Lost Falls. Sure, if he'd stayed he'd have had the very comfortable life of a working-class family. There would be grueling work, long hours and mindless tedium. A commitment to a business that needed to be open seven days a week, 362 days of the year.

And there would have been Claire….

That had been the hitch in his plans. She might have offset the compromise he'd have had to make if he'd chosen to stay. But he was eager enough to want to sow a few wild oats, young enough to question if what he really felt for Claire was love.

He still didn't know. He wondered sometimes if he'd ever know what love was. If he'd ever know when it was "right."

In the intervening years he'd been so busy putting everything in place that he'd only toyed with casual relationships. He'd surfed in Maui and skied in Aspen, but he'd never found a woman to share his adventures with. He was always around people, in business meetings with clients and glad-handing his way through L.A.'s most exclusive bars, yet he always felt as if he was alone. Even when he took a woman to dinner, or bought her a drink. Or took her home.

Zoey jumped down from the window and brushed against his pants, interrupting his thoughts to do figure eights around his legs. He pushed back from the table, picked her up and stroked her. She purred, stretching her neck so he could scratch under her chin. He indulged her, then tucked her into the crook of his arm, as if she were Claire's beloved baby, and absently wandered over to the calendar tacked on the wall beside the telephone.

Two days until his mother's afternoon funeral.

A week, at most, to spend alone with Claire until his sisters all went home.

He flicked a thumb over Monday, May 18. He'd probably move out that day and move back into his mother's place.

That was the day Claire would have lunch with Kate and meet with the Lost Falls playground committee at seven. Damn, she had a full calendar. Aside from all the luncheon dates she had penciled in, there were meeting times for the library and the Summer Social committees. There were evenings devoted to adult interest classes. Gardening with Perennials and Faux Painting Techniques. One weekend had a notation for the Restview Nursing Home. There were five dates on the calendar to remind her of upcoming birthdays and anniversaries. The Colton wedding was scheduled for June 29, and the Bliss baby shower was scheduled for the thirtieth.

She had a full life. Without him.

He stroked the cat's fur, inexplicably bothered to realize that Claire was still alone and obviously content. She had a community she cared for, and one that obviously cared for her.

She'd made it without him, her own way, just as he'd known she would. He was proud of her—and yet seeing that she was busy, that she didn't need him anymore, stung.

The temperatures were moderate and the sun shone for Ella Starnes's funeral. The church was full to overflowing, and Claire hovered near the back, debating where she should squeeze in. She'd just given Courtney's baby a bottle and offered a packet of tissues to Mindy who had already run out.

Feeling a light touch on her arm, she turned to see Hunter's sister. Beth's eyes were swollen, but steady. Hunter stood behind her, at her shoulder. His features were strained. "We'd like you to sit with us, Claire," Beth said. "The first two pews are reserved."

"Oh, no," she protested. "I—"

"You're like part of the family, Claire," Hunter interrupted.

Claire immediately guessed he'd been coerced into the decision. "But—"

"No sense you sitting alone. Besides," he said gruffly, "the girls won't have it any other way."

Claire sent him a sharp look, then waffled. She didn't want to give anyone in Lost Falls the wrong impression. Certainly not where Hunter was concerned. Then again, everyone knew that their broken romance had not severed her ties with his family. "I don't want to be in the way, or intrude, or…" Claire trailed off.

Hunter's eyes softened, and she recognized a bit of the old fondness, the old appreciation in their depths. "Nobody thought you were in the way when you were sending over cookies, or picking up Mom's prescriptions, or shoveling her drive. You may have thought I was intruding when you offered to put me up," he said, a sardonic grin pulling at the taut corners of his mouth, "but you never came out and said it. Not exactly."

Claire bit back her own conciliatory smile. Spending the last three days in the same house with Hunter was having an effect on her—an effect she didn't want to consider.

"Come on, Claire," Beth coaxed. "There's room."

"Okay," she agreed reluctantly. "I'll take the back corner."

"Whatever works," Beth said, her eyes going misty as she gave Claire a hug. "We just want you with us."

Claire returned the embrace and looked over Beth's shoulder, conscious only of Hunter's dark suit, his crisp white shirt. She could smell his aftershave and the faint scent of the soap she'd had in her bathroom. It was strange to think of them sharing so much as a bar of soap, particularly after all these years.

It was stranger still to be hugging his sister when she wanted to be hugging him. She'd given him her condolences, but she found herself wanting to comfort him. To be able to talk about how he felt about losing his mother and coming home after all these years.

Yet for the last two days they had waltzed around each other. Politely. Each going about their own schedules, with all their unfinished business unaddressed. With all the things they should have shared unsaid.

Beth patted Claire on the back as if she were her baby sister and not just a family friend, then stepped away. With her arms feeling curiously empty, Claire looked up at Hunter. The most peculiar expression crossed his features, making her wonder if he expected her to step right up and give him a hug, too.

The moment lapsed.

She couldn't bring herself to do it, not in front of all these onlookers, mourners at his mother's funeral, people who would speculate if Claire and Hunter still had something going. So she nodded at him, ducking her chin and turning away to make a solitary pilgrimage down the aisle to the spot that the Starnes family had kept for her.

There was the lightest touch on her forearm, stopping her. She did a stutter step, reeling herself back in, and feeling the same old electricity shoot back up her arm before zeroing in on her heart. When Hunter's touch lingered, she vaguely realized he didn't want to let her go.

"Claire?" Hunter rasped, the burnished color of his eyes turbulent with unspent emotion. "Thanks. No matter what, you've always been there for me, too."

Claire's throat went tight, and rather than choke over an answer or risk saying something stupid, she mouthed, "That's okay."

So she'd sat with the family, although Hunter sat ahead of her in the first row, two spots to her left. It had been an agonizing hour. For no matter how hard she tried to concentrate on the eulogy or Ella's favorite hymns, her mind drifted over to Hunter, her eyes taking in his chiseled profile.

He sat erect, his features arranged in a stoic mask, but Claire knew he was a wreck on the inside. He'd loved his mother dearly. He had held her outspoken opinions in high regard—even if he hadn't always agreed with them.

It occurred to Claire that Ella was probably having a good laugh over this one. She'd finally gotten Claire into the family one way or another, even if it had taken a funeral to do so. It had been Ella who had offered Claire the most support that first day, when Hunter had walked out.

"The boy's got a twenty-something brain," she'd said. "It's addled." She'd nodded, as if her advice was sage and true.

"Don't reckon he knows yet what he's given up. Just don't you give up on him, Claire," she'd chided.

But maybe it had been her mother who had unwittingly encouraged Claire to move on, by the things she said.

Don't make the same mistake I did, Claire, loving a man who can never be there for you.

You never came from a good enough family for him, Claire. He just felt sorry for you, that's all.

Her mother had grown into a sad, embittered woman—the exact opposite of Ella. Yet the two had been best friends for the better part of their lives.

The Dents and the Starneses, living side by side in a small town—an affluent house next to a poor one—had maintained a companionable friendship. Claire's mother had done the Starnes's ironing while she watched her favorite soap operas in the afternoon, and Ella repaid her with dusty, packaged treats from the gas-station snack shop. Hunter's father put in a huge garden, and sometimes Claire's mother watered it, prompting Ella to give them the produce to tide them over in the summer.

Claire had a lifetime of memories invested in Hunter and his family. Yet this event was the ending and the beginning all rolled into one. One Starnes family member had left her while another had come back, however briefly.

She boldly glanced over at Hunter, suddenly not caring who saw or made note of her scrutiny. A scruffy bit of his hair splayed over the collar of his dress shirt. The cords in his neck stood out, and the muscle along his jaw was iron hard, as if he was fighting any display of emotion. His forehead furrowed and his eyelids shuttered closed, squeezing tight. His head dropped a fraction of an inch, his square chin pulling back. When he opened his eyes again Claire detected the tiniest flecks of moisture on his lashes.

Her heart turned inside out, and her throat went raw and scratchy.

Yes, it was the hardest thing in the world to sit at his mother's funeral and know that she still loved him and that she couldn't comfort him the way she longed to.

Chapter Five

"What? You aren't hurrying out for work this morning?" Hunter asked, his gaze leisurely taking in Claire's drawstring sweats and scoop-neck top before drifting lower to stare at her bare toes.

She ambled over to the coffeepot, conscious of his scrutiny. "I've got an appointment to show a house at ten. No hurry." She picked up her favorite mug, then poured herself a cup of coffee. Zoey, at her feet, happily lapped at another can of gourmet tuna.

When she turned around, Hunter uncovered a plate of doughnuts, arching an eyebrow at her. "I figured you'd cut out of here and avoid me like you usually do, so I stopped by the bakery. Figured that would lure you into staying for a few extra minutes."

Claire eyed the doughnuts. "I'm not avoiding you."

"Sure you are." He nudged the doughnuts in her direction and offered up the most persuasive grin. "Come on. Sit down. I got glazed because I know they're your favorite."

Unease trickled through her. She didn't want him to do or say anything reminiscent of the "good old days." "Just so you know," she said, "I discovered Bavarian cream filled—and that's running neck and neck with glazed right now."

He laughed. "We'll do those tomorrow. My treat." He leaned back and stretched out his long, muscular legs. Using the toe of his shoe, he pushed back the adjoining chair. "Have a seat," he invited.

She drew back, as if she were impressed. "My. Those are some manners. You learned them in the big city, did you?"

"You'd be surprised at what I learned in the big city."

Innuendo and suggestion hung heavily in the air. All the things he had done; all the things she had not.

"Maybe I don't care to know," she retorted, plopping into the chair and going eye-to-eye with him.

"Good. 'Cause I wasn't going to tell you anyway."

In spite of her resolve not to, she laughed. A warm, fuzzy feeling suffused her, and she began to feel as she had when they were growing up and he was her best friend, her confidant. "You know what? We sound like we're twelve again."

"What's wrong with that? I loved making you worm the secrets out of me. I'd probably still like it. You never could stand not to be in on a secret."

She picked up a doughnut and pulled off a piece, first licking a drop of glaze from her fingers. "But you don't have secrets anymore. Your life's an open book."

"Really?" He leaned forward, wedging his elbows on the table. "Is that what you think?

"Mmm." Claire took a bite of the doughnut, silently admitting that the only thing she was hungry for was flirting with him again. "You're the small-town kid who came home as the fair-haired boy."

"That's it? In a nutshell."

She shrugged. "Okay. You made a name for yourself, and a ton of money. You wheel and deal and have friends whose names regularly pop up on the *Forbes* list. You have experiences that make our lives in Lost Falls look as dull as dishwater."

He dismissed her statement. "You have plenty of excitement around here. It's just a different kind."

"Yes, we sit around and watch the grass grow."

"Claire. According to *that*—" he tilted his head in the direction of her wall calendar "—you have a pretty busy life and a lot going on."

"We try," she said, her voice dropping a bit. She felt as if she'd been chastised for poking fun at the life she'd chosen.

"I saw Charlie McGowan yesterday. Said he's got two sets of twins."

Claire smiled and beat back a burst of envy, thinking of their double blessing. "I know. They couldn't have children for eleven years and then they discovered some old fertility rite."

"Fertility drugs?"

"No. Fertility *rite*. As in—" her lower lip wiggled, thinking of what Joan McGowan had told her "—private joke."

"Ah…"

To her relief he didn't ask.

"And your brothers?" he said, changing the subject. "What about them? I suppose they've got a dozen kids between them."

Claire paused, wondering what she needed to say, and how much she could get away with. "Jess and Jeremy are both married. Jess has four kids and Jeremy and his wife are expecting. They both ended up in Colorado. I don't see them much. Mom kind of…well, you know…wore them out around here. She was always so worried they'd turn out like Daddy—or Adam—that she was always on their case."

Hunter nodded. "And how's your oldest brother?" he asked carefully.

"He turned up in Texas. Your mom didn't tell you?"

"She wasn't, um, the best about filling me in on the news. She told me things like what Edith Jenkins put in her potato salad or where they planted the new pine trees at the school. But she stayed pretty silent about you and your family." So. Ella stayed silent about each of them, to each of them. Claire found that oddly significant. "Now Adam?" Hunter said. "*That* I would have wanted to know about."

"He had a pretty rough time of it," Claire admitted. "She probably didn't want to tell you that."

"Well, he ran off at sixteen," Hunter said, as if that explained the whole matter. "I remember the day he lit out, because I was in the driveway working on my bike. Your mom told him to rake the leaves in the backyard. He worked for about an hour, then he laid the rake against the shed and walked off into the sunset."

"He told me he hitched a ride with a trucker and made his way down to Texas," Claire confided. "The sad thing was, Mom made those boys work, but she never taught them how to have fun. A few years ago, just before she died, she said that it was the only way she knew how to keep them in line. Idle hands, wayward thoughts, that kind of thing."

"But your brothers were good kids, Claire."

"I know," she said, a bit of the old misery creeping into her soul. "But no matter how often I took their side, it didn't help."

"It wasn't your fault. She already had her mind made up to make them pay, Claire."

"But they were just little boys when Daddy left, Hunter," she said, unable to keep the pleading note from her voice. "Yet she blamed them for everything, things that weren't their fault."

"You don't have to say it. I remember how things were. She put you in the middle, whether you wanted to be or not."

Claire didn't address that. She'd always stood up for her brothers, and mothered them when her own mother couldn't. She'd gone to their basketball games and baked them cookies and bought them the jeans with the right label. But it had never been enough. She'd tried to hold it together for everyone—and that was part of the reason she'd stayed behind. To keep the home intact and care for her ailing, angry mother. "But Adam?" she said brightly. "He found somebody to give him a chance and got it together. He works on diesel engines now, for a big transport company in Dallas. I guess he's got a girlfriend. About time, him being two years older than me."

"You haven't seen him?"

Claire shook her head. "I thought he'd come back for Mom's funeral, but…"

"He could have come back for you."

Claire couldn't bring herself to say anything for a moment, because all she saw was irony. "Think about it," she said wryly. "All the men in my life leave me. I'm getting rather used to it by now."

Beth talked Claire into coming over to their house for dinner, and Hunter had to admit that there were moments he felt as if they were getting together just as they used to. Still, it had been difficult to be around his family while acting like he and Claire had happily come full circle and had put the high-school romance thing behind them.

He was having a heck of a time keeping up the charade, yet Claire seemed to manage it, and she blended in beautifully.

She stood in the den with eight-month-old Shannon on her hip, and looked over Courtney's shoulder at the address book on Ella's desk. "No," she said absently, affectionately stroking Shannon's bare foot, "I think *that* Snider is the one she went to high school with—and that Schneider," she went on, overemphasizing the *Sch,* "is the one she sold the tow truck to. They were business contacts, I'm sure of it."

"Thanks. Then I guess I won't need to let the tow truck people know," Courtney said, frowning. "I never realized how many people she and Daddy knew. I mean, I looked at this address book and was just stunned. I'll write as many as I can, but it's going to take longer than I imagined."

"Don't worry," Claire assured, straightening and giving Courtney a pat on the back. The baby, Shannon, peeked over Claire's shoulder, to roll twinkling blue eyes in Hunter's direction. "Contacting everyone may be impossible. Keep in mind your mother picked up a lot of new friends through her travels these past few years, and it complicated her address book."

Courtney shook her head, and put a big red *X* over the name. "Who would have thought my mother would climb the Mayan ruins and walk the cobblestone streets of London?"

"It was good for her," Claire assured. "She had her own life and she didn't sit around fussing about her kids having independent ones of their own. Seeing that was a good example for me."

Behind Claire, Hunter impulsively waved at the baby and made a face.

Shannon wriggled, determined to climb over Claire's shoulder and snag some time with him. "Ha-tah!" she crowed, flailing her arms.

Claire pivoted, her hand on Shannon's back. "Oh, Uncle Hunter. Are you what got her so excited?" she accused. "I finally get my hands on her, and you lure her away."

He laughed guiltily.

Shannon pitched forward, demanding that Hunter take her. "Gah-bah!" she squealed.

"Don't you dare give him my baby," Courtney complained, eyeing the way Claire struggled to keep her upright. "He spoils her. Last night, he gave her *ice cream*," she revealed, uttering the words as if they contained four particularly nasty letters instead of four scrumptious ingredients.

Claire laughed as Shannon's fat bottom bounced up and down on her forearm.

"Just a taste," Hunter defended, reaching for the baby before she catapulted out of Claire's arms. "Didn't hurt her one bit."

Claire nuzzled the baby's curls before reluctantly giving her up. Her eyelids drifted half-closed, as if she was memorizing the smell of baby powder and lotion. The gesture pulled at Hunter's heartstrings and made him feel like a heel, as if he was stealing something particularly precious away from her.

He should never have come in here. But the guys were out on the patio talking about the trials of putting gas grills together, and the girls were in the kitchen arguing over whether they should use cornstarch or flour in the gravy. Crud, he didn't belong anywhere. So he'd ambled off, looking for Claire.

Unfortunately he'd found her in a very maternal pose, one that turned a knife in the deepest part of his belly. He'd stood at that doorway for several minutes, listening to her talk with Courtney about who she should contact about their mother's fatal stroke and appreciating the way she held Shannon.

Claire loved babies. She gravitated to a baby the way a hummingbird gravitated to nectar. Her whole face changed whenever there was a baby around. She cuddled and talked to them and made them laugh and coo.

Claire was meant to be a mother and he distinctly remembered the day they'd once talked about the babies they'd have. Instead, today, they stood here separately, both single and childless. Even as they huddled together like a family, playing a push-pull act over someone else's child.

Hunter experienced a smattering of regret.

Ten years ago, he'd told himself that Claire would be okay, that she'd marry and have a dozen kids. Five years ago he'd told himself that she was just being picky and waiting for that one exceptional man to come into her life. Today he was utterly surprised and shocked that anyone, including him, had let a woman this desirable get away.

Claire would be the perfect housemate, wife and mother. He must have had oatmeal where his brains should have been.

Claire waggled Shannon's hand. "Oh? You don't like me so well, huh? Have to bribe you with ice cream and cookies to keep you, huh?"

"Don't you dare," Courtney warned, without looking up from the address book.

They all laughed. Still, Hunter detected a yearning in Claire that was tangible. She smiled and nibbled Shannon's fingertips, but her mouth trembled, her eyes were a tad too sparkly, her lashes damp.

It was obvious that Claire had a hole in her heart—one that a baby would fill.

He'd gift Claire with just about anything, for being his childhood friend and confidante, for being his mother's best companion in her last and final years. But a baby was something money couldn't buy and he couldn't give.

He wondered, vaguely, if she'd ever have children. It disturbed him deeply to think that it might never happen.

"Dinner's almost ready," Beth announced, coming into the den. "And Claire? Remember this?" She extended a china teapot, one that was delicately hand painted with cabbage roses and ivy. "Mom always said you admired it. I thought you might like to have it. You know, something more to dust."

"Oh, Beth…" Claire reached for it, then stopped herself. "Maybe one of the other girls? Or—" her gaze drifted back to him "—Hunter?"

"Oh, puh-lease," Hunter said, intentionally rolling his eyes. "Do I look like the tea and crumpets type?"

His sisters both laughed.

"No, you look like the energy-bar and bottled-water type," Claire said dryly, shaking her head as she accepted it. "You'd probably put this in the microwave and try to heat something in it."

"Ouch, that hurts!" He turned to his sisters. "Do you see? Do you see what this woman is really like? And I have been putting up with her for a week, in her house, on her terms, and I swear it has not been easy."

He looked from one unsympathetic face to another. But the truth was, he silently admitted, the week with Claire *had* been hell. She and all her tempting traits and taunting indifference had practically driven him to distraction. He couldn't count the number of times he'd wanted to toss her on the bed and say, "Let's play house one more time, for old times' sake." But he couldn't. Because he knew full well where that would lead—right back into a truckload of trouble.

"We're all leaving tomorrow," Beth announced without batting an eyelash. "So you've got the house back. All to yourself. I'm certain Claire will be happy to be rid of you."

He glanced over at Claire, suddenly uncomfortable that he hadn't told her. A trace of surprise hovered behind her eyes and on her forehead, but she quickly covered it. Her mouth firmed. The girls didn't see it. But he did.

"You mean he won't be cluttering up my kitchen anymore?" she offhandedly asked.

"Don't count on it," Beth said. "We're leaving him behind to clear up the estate."

"He'll probably whine and beg for free food," Courtney put in. "Or he'll want you to iron his shirts."

"Wait a minute," he argued. "I've learned how to iron my shirts, but I'll admit I've gotten particularly attached to Claire's coffeemaker."

Both his sisters groaned.

"So I'll loan it to you," Claire offered. She lifted the teapot. "I'll do tea."

Hunter feigned hurt. "But I thought we had some rather stimulating breakfast conversation."

Claire nonchalantly lifted a shoulder. "Mmm, yes, but you never bothered to see what I could do at night."

Beth choked; Courtney snickered.

"I meant—that, that—" Claire stammered, trying to explain.

"Yes?" he said. "Do clarify."

"That we never *talked*. Over dinner. Or—or…"

"We talked in your bedroom that first night," he reminded.

"I was *showing* you the room!"

"And you did it so well."

"Well, I didn't want you to just throw your clothes on the floor!"

He lifted both eyebrows. His sisters laughed.

"Because I'd cleaned out that closet," Claire said primly.

"And you made a big deal over that bedspread, too," he reminded.

"It's *new*. I didn't want it all rumpled."

"Yes, I do remember you said something about that…."

Claire rolled her eyes to look at Beth. "He's exaggerating, and you know it."

Beth wiped at the corner of her mouth, her grin barely fading. "I know. But you two? You'll never change. Put you in the same room and stuff just happens. You play off of each other like two musicians on a keyboard."

Courtney tilted her head. "But right now? Forget the keyboard and put that baby in a high chair, please. Today's the day we introduce strained peas."

"Really? Well, yes, ma'am. Wouldn't want this little waif to miss out on her golden opportunity for six strained peas." Hunter winked, backing out of the room.

"He's actually taking orders from you now?" Beth looked at her sister in disbelief.

Courtney shrugged. "He owes me. For all those years he pulled my ponytail and made fun of my skinny legs. But he's still got a mouth that has to have the last word."

"He always was a handful," Beth admitted. "But—" she turned to Claire, looking at her sympathetically, as if she'd be open to anything Claire wanted to reveal "—I hope he behaved himself at your house, Claire."

"Beth, the man's thirty-five years old. He *knows* how to behave."

"Really? You think so?" Beth appeared slightly disappointed when Claire didn't say more. "Well, he's got every material possession he's ever wanted. He's spoiled rotten. I worried, imagining him over at your house, complaining about the paper napkins or being without cable or not having the *New York Times* at his elbow."

"Beth's right. He's not happy," Courtney put in decisively. "You ever notice that it's either business or it's by-himself?"

"It's true," Beth confided to Claire, lowering her voice.

"He's dated a couple of women, but it was never anything serious. Not much more than companionable. Certainly not passionate." She let a second slip away. "Not after you, Claire."

Claire blinked, and heat suffused her cheeks. She looked from one sister to the other. She hadn't expected this. Hadn't even wanted it. For a moment, she wasn't even sure what they were trying to tell her.

To go after him, no matter what? Or leave him floundering with his confounded business aspirations?

"I'd take that as a compliment, Claire," Courtney encouraged. "You ought to think about it."

"I…am." But Claire knew she sounded anything but convinced.

Beth leaned closer. "Frankly, I think he's miserable and doesn't even know it."

"And you ever notice how he seems uncomfortable with us, because we're all married?" Courtney asked, raising both eyebrows. "He ends up playing with the kids. I'm beginning to think maybe he's just scared of commitment. He certainly doesn't want to talk about mortgage rates or houses in the suburbs."

Claire, beginning to feel a bit uncomfortable herself, took a step back.

"He's not scared of commitment," Beth suggested to her sister. "He wants to put it in a time frame. And we all know that's not possible." Beth's fingers settled on Claire's wrist, drawing her back into the inner circle of Starnes sisters. "Listen, Claire, it'll be good for him to be here for a while, without us. Without thinking about business all the time. You'll look after him, won't you?"

"Well…I…"

"Say you'll do it, Claire," Courtney urged. "He needs some looking after. I worry about him, too."

"He's a grown man," Claire protested.

"Yes, and he's only going to grow into an older, grumpier, more inflexible man if someone doesn't intervene," Beth said. "And right now, that someone is you. Promise me you'll talk to him, tell him to kick back a while and smell the roses—or whatever it is men do when they settle down and relax and forget about work."

"That's it, Claire," Courtney urged. "Spend some time with him. He needs you right now. I know he does."

Claire looked from one sister to the other, and simply had no idea what to say.

Chapter Six

Claire watched Hunter move his suitcases to the back door, and a ripple of regret coursed through her. She couldn't believe his sisters had been dead serious about her looking out for him. Or having a heart-to-heart talk with him. Or even spending some time with him.

Feeling cornered, even though there had been a door at her back, she'd fumbled through some offhand answers. She'd joked her way through the situation, and they'd all laughed.

But the answer had come to her in the middle of the night, when she was alone in her bed and her emotions were running amuck.

He's a big boy, he can take care of himself.

Now *that's* what she should have said. Instead she'd stammered out some pitiable reply—she couldn't even remember what—and Beth and Courtney had both hugged her and laughed and said something about her being the funniest, dearest thing, just like their own sister.

Well, she hadn't been feeling "funny" or "dear," not when she was silently cussing Hunter out in the middle of the night, in the privacy of her own bedroom. That evening she had barely been able to look at him across the dinner table, thinking of what his sisters had said and wondering, exactly, what they meant.

Hunter had been oblivious to his sisters' requests. He told stories about his experiences in San Francisco, about deals he'd made in a fast-food franchise in Sacramento and on the ski slopes in Aspen. In between, the Starnes girls talked about their kids, the merits of wallpapering their nurseries with ducks or cartoon characters and the value of intramural versus competitive sports.

Claire had sat there and vowed she never wanted to be with this family again, even as much as she loved them. It was just too stressful. She didn't have any wild tale, so the closest she'd come was the story of selling the six-bedroom house with the spa, the sauna, the pool and only one drawer in the kitchen. She couldn't elaborate about moving into a nice little three-bedroom house in the suburbs, her efforts with scrapbooking to record her family's milestones, or her trials of scheduling meals around soccer games and Little League.

Compared to them, her life seemed middle-of-the-road. She didn't have a "better half" to boast about or complain about. She didn't have little ones to brag about or worry about.

It all made her wonder why she couldn't just make compromises and get married? Even if she had to settle for someone.

Someone other than Hunter, of course.

Because, she told herself sadly, looking at his paired luggage, no one made her blood pulse quite as fast, or put a flutter in her middle, or a retort to her lips. No one. Not ever. Not like Hunter.

She wanted to put her head down on the table and cry. She wanted to sob and beg him not to go, to tell him that she loved him, that she'd always loved him. She ached to tell him that the past week had been like a reprieve to her soul, that she had captured every moment he'd shared with her and memorized them, playing them over and over again like a tape inside her head. Cherishing each word he'd uttered. Imprinting the scrawl of his handwriting or the scent of his aftershave.

On the inside, her heart was weeping. But, on the outside, where it showed, she told herself that there was only one thing she could have—and there was only one thing he couldn't rip out of her—and that was pride.

She'd maintain her pride, no matter what.

Her mother always claimed Claire had too much pride; she said it would be her daughter's downfall someday. Maybe she was right. But this time, seeing how determined Hunter was to return to his solitary life, there didn't seem to be anything left but pride.

So she'd salvage that, look him squarely in the eye and say goodbye. From this day forward she'd see him only occasionally, when he used the back door to the house. Maybe she'd see him get the mail, or come in from his early-morning run. But they'd never share a cup of coffee from the same pot again, or linger over yogurt and laugh about the good old days.

Zoey would have to go back to regular tuna. And Claire would have to go back to her regular life.

Hunter intended to leave. One more time. That's why his suitcases were sitting at the back door.

"Well, I think that's about all of it," he said, coming into the kitchen. He paused, peering at Claire. "You okay?"

"I…" She drifted off. "Was just thinking. About your sisters. And how good they were to me last night. And wondering when I'll see them again."

Hunter pulled out a chair to sit opposite her. "You know they won't be strangers."

"I know. It's all this change. That's all." She idly folded over a corner of the paper napkin she'd used for breakfast. "But their kids will probably grow a foot, and Shannon will probably be stringing whole sentences together by the time I see her again. She'll be peddling a bicycle or driving a car, not toddling." She offered up a half laugh. "Provided Courtney sees fit to put wheels under her daughter." He snorted. "Anyway, I'm going to miss that toddling stage, and I love that."

"Is there anything keeping you from going and seeing *them?*" he asked. "You know you're always welcome. And Minnesota isn't on the other side of the world."

Claire's gaze drifted over to Hunter. "No. You're right. There's not a thing holding me back." She lifted a shoulder. "Maybe someday."

Silence filled the room, the inevitable parting had left them speechless once again.

"You'd be a great mom, Claire," he said finally, slowly, carefully. "Maybe someday you ought to think about that."

"Oh…I have. But…"

"Yes?"

"I have this old-fashioned idea that the right man has to be part of it."

"There's a lot of single parents around," he pointed out, pensively scraping his thumbnail over an old nick in the table. "It wouldn't be out of the ordinary."

"I know. And a lot of them do a remarkable job of parenting. But…I grew up with a dad who was never around, Hunter. I wouldn't want to intentionally do that to a child."

He nodded. "But if it's the money—"

"No," she said quickly. "It isn't. It's the emotion. Sure, I could adopt, or…" She drifted off. "Well, you know, there are other ways. Science has done an incredible job of offering us options. And a lot of women simply choose to get themselves pregnant." His eyebrow lifted, then arched. "But I'm not one of those."

They sat there for some moments.

"It was just seeing you with Shannon last night…." he said finally.

"She's a cutie, isn't she?" Claire forced a smile to her lips. "Don't worry about me, Hunter," she said, patting the back of his hand as if she herself were indifferent to the matter. "If it's meant to be, it's meant to be. Maybe someday a guy will come along and sweep me off my feet, and I'll wind up having a dozen kids yet. Stranger things have happened."

Hunter sucked in a breath and rolled his eyes. "Now don't go overboard, Claire."

She laughed. But it was a nervous response, to hide her growing anxiety. It was quickly becoming apparent that each second she spent with him would be one of her last. She didn't want to talk about indelicate matters or deep, heavy issues because she knew none of them would be resolved. Not ever.

"Well? You're probably happy to have me out of your house."

She raised her head, half-afraid he could see the sorrow in her eyes, the regret in her soul. She tried to jest, to let truth linger below the surface. "Hey. I wasn't happy about you moving in. But…it's going to take some getting used to, to realize your mom isn't next door. Having you here helped."

"So it wasn't so bad, huh? Having me around."

"Not like I thought."

He leaned across the table, his fingertip tracing a path over the back of her hand and onto her wrist. "I owe you, Claire. For putting me up. And putting up with me. And putting our differences…well…aside. For the time being."

"Don't be ridiculous. You don't owe me anything." But her throat started to constrict, making Claire strangle over the words. "It was the…neighborly thing to do, that's all."

"Even so, it meant a lot." He paused, as if gauging how far he could go. Then he abruptly patted her hand. "Dinner out? Sometime this week, maybe? My way of repaying all your hospitality."

Claire debated, thinking of how she'd promised his sisters, yet knowing it would be a mistake to let him have so much as an hour of her undivided attention. Still, she reminded herself, she could have him again, if only for an evening.

But his intentions were clear; he was moving on. The time he spent in Lost Falls would have one purpose only—to tie up loose ends.

And she wasn't one of them.

"I don't think so, Hunter," she replied carefully. "You've seen my calendar. I've got a lot going on, and—"

He pushed back from the table, rising from the chair to brush a kiss across her cheek. He lingered, longer than he needed to, his face hovering near hers, his freshly shaven cheek brushing against a few wispy hairs near her temple. Her eyes drifted closed; she couldn't bear to look at him, feeling him close to her was enough.

His palm smoothed her hair away from her face. "Thanks, Claire," he said, his voice going husky. "For everything."

Then he turned and walked out the door.

Claire should have offered up the typical Lost Falls reply: "Anytime." But she couldn't bring herself to say it.

* * *

Claire took the lid off the container from the deli and reminded herself she was back to eating alone. Takeout for one. From here on out, she was back to eating single servings of soup or sandwiches she cut in half.

She'd worked as long as she possibly could today. She'd cleaned off her desk and made every phone call she needed to make. She'd done everything she could to avoid coming home to an empty house and reminders of Hunter.

Instead of putting things aright in her guest bedroom—not that she was picky, but Hunter had moved the vase, put the alarm clock on the wrong side of the nightstand and left a wrinkle in the bedspread—she shut the door to the room. It would be best to just avoid cleaning up after him for a few days. At least until the nagging memories began to subside.

She kept seeing snippets of him inside that dratted room. The way he leaned close to his reflection in the mirror as he knotted his tie. Or the way he sat on the edge of the bed to put on his shoes. Or the way she'd caught him, his elbow propped on the sill, gazing out the window—at the tree where they'd once fashioned a tree house from scrap lumber and not a lot of ingenuity.

It had been their first home together, she thought absurdly. A place where they'd looked up at the stars, and had broken a cookie in half on a hot afternoon and imagined they were languishing over a gourmet meal. That first little tree house had been crude, and it had been fashioned from castoffs…but it had been theirs.

It was going to take some time, she told herself, as she stared at the hard-boiled egg on her tossed salad.

What? She hated egg in her salad! Had she had a lapse of consciousness when she'd filled the tray? she silently berated herself. It was Hunter who loved egg in his salad. For years she had given him hers.

She took the dinner salad over to the sink, near the window that faced the Starnes's house and decisively picked the egg off. It was going right where it belonged. In the disposal.

That, and the memories, too.

Then she looked up and saw him, a flash of color going past the kitchen window.

He looked busy. As if he was going on with his life and about his business.

She turned the water on full force and directed her energy there.

He probably didn't eat right, a little voice inside her head suggested.

With her finger on the switch, she doggedly snapped on the disposal.

"So what?" she asked herself; it wasn't any of her affair.

It wasn't any of her affair? Oh, but they'd had that, the same little voice reminded. They'd had innocence and more. They'd had fervent, driving passion. Intense love. A love that had eaten them up, made them whole, then sliced them down the middle with all the pain and hurt of separation.

"But you're the only one with egg on your face," the voice taunted. "For loving a man who can't love you back."

A shudder went through her, and she wished with all her heart that she could stop thinking of Hunter. She glanced at the ravaged salad. She couldn't even think of eating. She had no desire to eat. Her mind was elsewhere.

It was on Hunter.

And her hunger pangs had nothing to do with food whatsoever.

She scooped the container of salad up and walked over to

the garbage can like a woman on a mission. She flipped the lid and poised the salad over it. Then the phone rang. She hesitated for the briefest of moments.

"Hello?"

"Claire?"

"Yes?" Her heart started thrumming and her voice went breathless.

"I'm having a time of it. Can't find a thing. I got steaks for tonight, and I can't find the tongs. Can't even find the broiling pan."

"Try the drawer next to the stove. Your mom kept her cooking utensils there."

"I already looked."

"In the back?"

"Well…"

She could hear the clatter, the shuffling. "Try the back porch, then. She put a lot of stuff she didn't use very often out there."

"Have you *seen* that room?" he asked. "It's going to take me a week to figure out how she organized it."

"It's probably next to the grill. She kept the grill covered, for when the girls came to visit. Look there."

"Claire," he implored. "Help. Come on. Can you come over? I've got these humongous steaks. They looked so good, I bought extra."

She waffled, thinking of the promise she had made his sisters. "I thought you wanted to be on your own."

"I never said that."

"But—"

"I didn't want to be in your way, or underfoot, and this house is empty…." An awkward silence ensued. "I got a lot of business done today, but my night is free…and I'm kind of wandering around here like I don't know what to do next. I could use a little help, a little direction."

"Hunter, you haven't needed direction in your life in the last twenty years."

"Maybe not. But I need it now."

Claire stared at the salad she'd been ready to dump. She pulled it back from its precarious angle. "I've got a salad," she said. "But it doesn't have egg on it."

"Too much cholesterol," he said, and she could hear the smile in his voice. "I gave up eggs in my salad."

"You did?" She drew the carton safely back against her, grateful she didn't pitch the whole mess. "So we could split what I've got."

"The back door's open, Claire," he said, a trace of suggestion in his voice. "You know the way over."

"Give me two minutes."

Chapter Seven

But the truth was, it probably took her less than that to cross the drive and let herself into the house.

"Found 'em," Hunter announced, the moment she walked in the door, "and they were right where you said they'd be."

"So you don't need me over here after all?"

He hesitated. "No. I do." He eyed the deli container. "You're bringing the salad. And I had more steak than I could eat." He paused briefly. "Claire, this is my first night back in the house—alone—and it seemed kind of empty." A second slipped away. "Know what I mean?"

She got a funny little feeling behind her breastbone. "I know exactly what you mean, Hunter." She came into the room, and slid the container on the table. She ached to put her arms around him, but she didn't dare. Doing so would be asking for trouble. "It will get easier," she said gently. "It's always a letdown after people go home."

She moved to the cupboard to get two place settings. Keeping her hands busy meant she could avoid his searching gaze. She intentionally put her back to him, and reached for two glasses, but she felt him behind her…and then his hands settled on her shoulders.

"With your mom?" he inquired softly. "How was it?"

"Rough," she admitted, forcing the catch from her voice.

"I almost came back."

"You did?"

"Mmm-hmm." His fingers kneaded the tension from her shoulders. "I even checked out the flights. But…"

"Yes?"

"I thought I might be one more burden. I wasn't sure if you wanted that, not at that time."

Claire let her head drop a fraction of an inch, and she winched her eyes closed, grateful he couldn't see her indecision. "I don't know that it would have been a burden, Hunter. Because it was totally different for me when my mom died. It was…" She paused, unsure she could say it. "…a relief." She straightened. "I know that sounds terrible."

"No. It doesn't." His hands stopped moving, a mere comforting weight on her shoulders.

"I loved her…and I know she wanted the best for me, and my brothers…but…"

"She couldn't let go of the past."

"No. She was so hell-bent that we were not going to repeat her mistakes, or my father's, that it ate her up. She spent her life telling us how we could do better, be better."

His palms slipped down her arms, then he circled her middle, encompassing her in a tight, compassionate hold.

She leaned back against Hunter, absorbing his heat. "For me," she continued, "after my mom was gone, it was relief and regret all mixed up together. For the life we should have had as a family, for the things we could have been to each other." His chin settled against the side of her temple, his warm breath tickling her cheek.

"You didn't have to stay," he said finally, his arms tightening even more.

"Yeah. I did." Claire stared straight ahead, at the satin finish on the cabinets. "She didn't have anyone else."

They stood there for some moments, each wrapped up in the past, and all it had cost them.

"Mom's estate is in pretty good shape," he said finally, loosening his hold on her and rolling to the side to wedge his hips against the counter and face her. "But it will still take a while to sort out. The girls were pretty clear about what they wanted and what they didn't. That made it easier, especially because everyone was amicable. But then, Beth sat us down that first night and pointed out it was more important for us to have each other. More than anything Mom or Dad had accumulated."

Claire offered up an appreciative laugh. "That Beth," she said. "She always took her role as the oldest seriously. I can see her as the matriarch of a large and extended family."

"Mmm, and I feel like she's looking over my shoulder. So if I mess up on this…" He drifted off, lifting both shoulders.

"The house? You're going to sell it?"

A smile tugged at his lips. "I don't know. Want the listing?"

"No," she denied. "I'm more interested in good neighbors."

He chuckled. "Well, you're going to have me for a while. We started looking at all the stuff to be taken care of…and the truth is Mom and Dad had more investments than I imagined. There's a lot of property. And the cars. I think we're going to leave the house till the last. So we'll have a place, if any of us need it."

"That's probably best."

"I started sifting through things today. Thinking that I would systematically take care of everything."

"Yes?"

"I was overwhelmed," he said. "I have to stop and consider. What Mom would have wanted. What the girls would want. What Dad would have said. What I think is best."

"It'll be like that for a while, Hunter," she said softly.

"I thought I'd take care of everything and be out of here, but…" He trailed off. "I may be here awhile. Longer than I thought." Hope and despair clashed. Hunter was going to be here longer than he'd originally planned, but he was also determined to leave. "But knowing you're here…it helps."

"Hunter—"

"No. Let me say it. I think I botched it this morning. I said thank you. But I meant thanks for being here for me. You always come through, Claire. Always."

Claire recoiled, realizing she didn't want praise. She didn't need it, not for the little she'd done. "Hunter…it was something I wanted to do for your whole family. I mean—and I don't want to hurt your feelings—but it wasn't just for you. It was for your mom. And your family. And it was about being neighbors."

He gave her a sideways glance, as if he was debating the truth of her words. "Yeah. Right."

"We've got a lot of history, Hunter. But I'm older and wiser. I want something else now, something we both realized you weren't able to give me a dozen years ago." He inclined his head, silently questioning her. "I want my own life and family, in this small town."

"You seeing someone, Claire?"

Inside, she flinched. She'd had a few casual dinners and twice as many god-awful blind dates since he'd left. Nothing had clicked. She'd even tried to *make* them work. But you couldn't make something happen when your heart wasn't in it. "Not right now," she replied, half-embarrassed to admit no one else had chosen to pursue her with the zeal, the intensity, Hunter'd once had. Of course, part of the problem had been that she'd always compared those men to Hunter.

"So how are you going to do this family thing, without someone waiting in the wings?"

She lifted a shoulder. "I don't know. But time's running out for me. That old biological ticktock, you know."

Hunter's gaze dropped to her throat, to the V of her blouse. "I thought about that today. What you said. If anyone could raise a child alone, you could, Claire."

"Oh, probably not. My mom pretty much did that and look how I turned out."

He chuckled. "I'm looking, I'm looking. And, frankly, I think you turned out pretty damn good."

"Flattery will get you absolutely nowhere."

"But you'd make a great mother, Claire."

"Thanks, but…to tell you the truth, I'm getting the impression it's not in the cards."

"Oh, c'mon."

"No. I mean it." She reached for the tea towel that was lying on the countertop beside her. She folded it, matching the corners. "I had a birthday six months ago—"

"January 29," he said automatically.

"And my doctor kindly reminded me that I'm not getting any younger. The risks are going up. And the chances of me getting pregnant are going down." She rolled her eyes. "That was kind of personal. I suppose I shouldn't have told you that. But it's the reason why… I'm not sure it's ever going to happen."

His eyes went dark, thoughtful, his expression kind. "Hey. You can tell me anything, remember?" He touched the pad of his forefinger to the tip of his tongue and extended it. She pressed her thumb against it and twisted. "Secrets and a wink," he recited, bending his wrist to hook his pinkie with hers, "only in words and not in ink."

Claire's little finger slowly slipped from Hunter's, the tip of her nail grazing the inside of the joint. "My. We haven't done that in a long time."

"I don't know what made me think of it. We used that as part of our secret code to get into the tree house."

"Until my little brothers found out and started copying us."

Both of them grew silent, remembering the good times of their childhood.

"So. Me, either," he said finally.

"Excuse me?"

"There isn't anyone I'm seeing, either."

"Oh? I'm surprised."

"I'm always busy with work. In fact, everything is work related. And the ladies out there? At least the ones I seem to pick? They're always more interested in corporate earnings or incentive programs. They intimately know every drink on the bar menu, but they don't know how to fix a pot roast or mashed potatoes." He paused. "The last time I bought a woman a drink, you know what she ordered?"

"Hmm?"

"Sex On The Beach."

Claire felt her irises widen.

"It's the name of a drink," he said hastily. "I swear."

"It was probably also an invitation," she said dryly.

He shrugged. "Not that I was interested."

"Yes, well, look at me. I don't know anything about…" She

hesitated. "Sex On The Beach, but I can fix a pot roast. And you walked away from that. Obviously that isn't what you want, either."

"Yeah, but…people change, Claire. Over the years. Things happen. Their ideas, their viewpoints change. They choose a path and follow it, then they live with the compromises—or the consequences."

"I think that says it all, Hunter. It may not be Sex On The Beach, but it doesn't have to be pot roast, either. Not for either of us."

He chuckled. "But we've got a lot of good history, don't we, Claire-bear?"

Warmth suffused her, and goose bumps popped up on her arms. No one had called her that in years. It had been Hunter's pet name for her. Hearing it again was poignant. "We do, Hunter," she said, nearly stumbling over the catch in her voice. "A lot of good memories."

"How about, tonight, it's just you and me and a backyard barbecue? We can talk until the stars come out, we can laugh until our sides hurt."

That sounded just like what Claire needed—and just what she'd been missing for the last few years.

So—in honor of Ella's memory—they set the table with her favorite dishes. While Hunter grilled the steaks, Claire cut a bouquet of flowers from Ella's garden and arranged them in a vase. They looked so nice that Hunter declared they needed to be bathed in candlelight. He found a matching pair of tapers and put one on either side of the arrangement.

"There," he breathed, drawing the match back before flicking his wrist to put out the flame. "Dinner for two."

A corner of Claire's heart lifted. It was the most romantic thing she'd ever been a part of.

Hunter didn't stop there, either, not with the table settings or the food. He carried the night with conversation. It was everything Claire had ever dreamed.

She came to know Hunter as an adult. She had observed his little quirks and habits in her house…but now she heard the way his voice lifted at the end of a punch line or deepened with wry remarks. She relished the way his deep, resonant laugh filled a room. She saw the glow in his eyes and the animation in his face when he talked about California, the people he worked with, the experiences he'd had.

He asked her about herself. He didn't dwell any longer on her trials with her mother and her brothers. Instead he asked her about the classes she took and the work she did at the real estate office. He asked her about clients and houses and real estate itself. He seemed interested in everything she'd done since they'd parted.

And the layers of separation, of resistance and reluctance, fell away. Claire told him all.

They strolled through Ella's garden and she told him why she'd decided to get her real estate license. They sat in the white-painted Adirondack chairs while the stars came out, and she told him about her first sale.

Later, he opened up bottles of hard lemonade. They sat there, their heads tilted back against the wood, looking up at the stars, with their fingers curled around cold, sweating glass.

Finally, Claire yawned.

"Must be after midnight," Hunter said. "You probably have to work tomorrow."

She couldn't help it; disappointment welled. She knew the precious, coveted time with him would soon be over. Tonight she'd been freed of all animosity and regret—for these few hours they'd gotten past it.

"I should go." She pushed the bottle back and stood, swaying slightly as she got to her feet.

"Hey." He caught her around the waist, steadying her. "Not much of a drinker, are you?"

"You've always known my blood was like pure springwater," she retorted. "And it hasn't changed. Two of those, on a hot night…" She drifted off, letting herself lean into him. "Well, I go a little weak in the knees, but I'll be fine."

He laughed, and she was so close, she could hear the source of his amusement spring from the center of his being, rattle through his chest and rumble through his lungs. The sound made her yearn.

"You've always been fine, Claire-bear."

"Shouldn't say that," she admonished, her voice dropping to a whisper. "You'll make me think this dinner thing, this heart-to-heart stuff, will become an everyday occurrence."

He kissed her lightly on the temple. She shifted, positioning herself comfortably against him, realizing he was more tender, more thoughtful, than he'd been in his youth. Her breasts flattened against the hard length of him, her belly pressed against his.

Her chin lifted, instinct making a move toward another of the passionate kisses they'd once shared. Her head tilted back and her eyelids went heavy. Everything went hazy, distorted. She saw only Hunter—even as she sensed something in him, something that told her he was drawing away.

His fingertips trailed up her arm, sliding beneath her hair. Then the pad of his thumb brushed the spot he'd kissed, and he smoothed the hair back from her head, tucking a couple of wispy strands behind her ear. "Let me walk you to your door," he offered softly.

"Mmm. You never did that growing up."

"We parted ways in the middle of the driveway. Eight steps your way, eight steps mine." They moved in unison to her back door, his hand on the small of her back. "Claire?"

"Yes?"

"Thanks for tonight. I…" He hesitated, and Claire moved up the first step, to put herself eye level with him. He was positively gorgeous in the moonlight. His cheekbones were reminiscent of carved alabaster, his hair dark and inviting. "Look, I'm going to be pretty busy the next few days. So…if you don't see me for a while…"

Dread pulsed in her middle, and a sick feeling washed over her. She'd hoped he'd just wanted to take his time, but, no, he was brushing her off again. Before she could get too close. Before she could let this night together mean more than it did, more than he wanted it to. "I understand," she said too quickly.

"I've just got all these appointments," he said. "At the bank, with the insurance, with the lawyers, and—"

"I said I understand. This was…just one more step…in moving on with our lives. So tonight we let go, and we let each other have a glimpse into what we do and who we are. It made sense—that's all. I don't expect anything more from it."

Claire's reply was nonchalant, her smile was fixed, but inside turmoil bubbled beneath her calm exterior. The bottom line was that if it took a lie—or a gross exaggeration—to protect her heart, she'd use it.

Chapter Eight

It had been three days. Just as he'd predicted, Hunter made himself scarce. From the deepest recesses of her kitchen Claire watched him come and go. He moved like a man whose focus consumed him. As if he had a case of tunnel vision so severe that it impaired his ability to look anywhere but ahead straight ahead. He left early in the morning and came home late at night. In between, Claire caught glimpses of him.

She wished he'd pop in, even if it was only to tell her that she'd left the garden hose on too long and given him a mess to walk through on his way to the garage. Or that he'd run out of milk and could he borrow some of hers? Or maybe he would bring over some gourmet tuna for Zoey, who had become cross and disgruntled ever since she'd been deprived of her treat and had started casting accusing glances in Claire's direction.

She would have settled for just about anything from Hunter. Even a wave. Or a beep of his car horn. Instead she had to content herself with noting everything about him from a respectful distance. How he left in the morning, his hair still damp from the shower. How he always walked out the door strapping his watch on as the screen door slammed behind him. How he always wore the casually professional look: dark slacks, loafers and a three-button golf shirt.

In her wildest fantasies, Claire imagined how those shirts would look mingled in the laundry with hers. Buttercup gold—the shirt that best reflected his hazel eyes—would mix with her buff-colored slacks. The marine-blue one would tumble with her jeans. The sooty black one that mimicked his textured dark hair would swish in the washer with her dress slacks and silky blouse.

Laundry would no longer be a chore; it would be a pleasure. For she'd know that every time he slipped a shirt out of the drawer it had been her hands that put it there. That he, and that shirt, would come home to her each day, every day.

The last night they'd spent together had been blissfully relaxing. They'd talked as if the past had never happened. As if the grueling years of enduring their separation had been wiped away.

Claire wondered if he would make a move to permanently repair their relationship if she forced the issue. She wondered if they could even last together, after everything that had happened. How much, really, had they changed?

She'd worn herself near through with thinking. About him, and her, and everything their lives would mean if they put them together and tried again.

In the three days since she'd last seen him, she'd neglected her work. She'd postponed making calls, and she'd missed a deadline to get a listing in the paper. She'd also pushed back an open house. Her lack of concentration and focus could only be attributed to one thing: Hunter Starnes and the mind-boggling effect he had on her.

What was she doing, she asked herself? She had built a life without him, and she couldn't let him disrupt it one more time. Besides, it had been three days and he'd made no attempt to see her, or call her, or be in contact with her.

So on the fourth day, she realigned her thinking and flung herself back into work.

When she came home late that night, Hunter's car squarely straddled their shared drive. She was tired enough to be equally pleased and annoyed.

She pulled her car directly in behind him, snapped off the ignition and tossed the keys in her purse. There. If she couldn't get in, he couldn't get out. One way or another, that ought to bring him around.

He'd either have to come and get her keys or sit out in the drive and honk his horn, waiting for her to move her car. Or, maybe he'd stop by with a grin and an apology.

Right now, she'd settle for just about anything. She simply needed to see him one more time.

Ten minutes later, a knock sounded at her back door.

"That didn't take long," she congratulated herself as she moved to open the door, simultaneously buttoning the front of her nightgown. Hunter was on the top step, an engaging smile on his face.

"This driveway's a tracking system," he drawled, his eyes fixed on her working fingers. "If you play it right, you can keep track of arrivals and departures—and you can interrupt them both."

"You're keeping track?"

"Mmm-hmm. Sometimes." His gaze slid over the shoulders of her light summer nightgown. "I know you put in a long day today, and I wanted to give you enough time to change into something comfortable. Of course, I didn't think you'd change into *that*."

Claire self-consciously rubbed her bare arms, knowing she wasn't wearing anything particularly provocative. The intimate apparel merely stirred his imagination. "You could have left me a note, and I'd have stopped over."

He lazily lifted a shoulder and leaned against the door frame. "That's okay. I wanted to surprise you. So—" he jerked a thumb over his shoulder "—you want me to move my car, so you can get into your garage?"

"Fifteen minutes ago, maybe. But now? Forget it. Leave it sit. Remember, though, you're at my mercy tomorrow morning."

The cool night air wafted between them, raising goose bumps on her upper arms, making her nipples, beneath her gown, go pebble hard. She suddenly wondered if her reaction showed. She wondered if Hunter noticed.

"You going to ask me in?" he wheedled. His mouth slowly, sensually, worked around the words, framing them.

Anticipation thrummed in Claire's veins. He looked so sexy standing there, his mischievous boyish eyes, his quirky smile. "And why would I do that?"

"Now, Claire. C'mon. Don't make this difficult. Why do you think a gentleman asks to come in at a late hour, on a weeknight?"

"I don't know. Why?"

"Because—" Hunter barely pulled his weight off the door frame before waggling a thick, white envelope in front of her "—he has something to give her."

Expectancy buoyed Claire. She loved surprises, and she loved being remembered. Maybe he'd unearthed some old clipping or some interesting mementos from the station.

"Come in," she invited, pushing the screen door open a little farther.

He grinned and stepped inside. As he moved past her and into the kitchen, Claire inhaled the dark, musky scent that clung to his clothes. "Can't believe I had to bribe you for an invitation," he good-naturedly groused.

"I'm not used to men coming over after dark."

He chuckled. "That's good. I suppose," he added as an afterthought.

Claire sighed, turning to look at him over her shoulder. "You realize that what I'm admitting is that I lead a very boring life."

"I seriously doubt that."

"So." Her fingertips trailed over the tabletop. "You want the table, the couch? What?" She halfway hoped that he'd steer her to the direction of the couch and invite her to sit beside him.

He paused and flicked a look toward the living room—and the steps that led to the upstairs bedrooms. He looked momentarily undecided. "Um…table's fine," he replied, slowly pulling out a chair.

Zoey, hearing Hunter's voice, trotted into the kitchen. She purred and stretched, rubbing against his leg. Claire experienced a pang of jealousy. Zoey got all the privileges, she thought insanely. The next thing she knew, the little feline would be sitting in his lap and purring in his ear.

"Want something to drink?" she offered.

"No, I'm fine," he said, absently reaching down to scratch Zoey behind the ears.

Just as she predicted, Zoey hopped in his lap and nuzzled his neck. "She's crazy about you," Claire observed.

"I have that effect on most females," he said lightly, "but

this time around I think it has something to do with the gourmet tuna."

Zoey purred louder, as if she understood.

Claire and Hunter exchanged looks and laughed.

He slid the envelope onto the table, and Claire slid into the
chair opposite him, curiously eyeing it.

"Now. For this…" he announced, taking a deep breath.
"Well, I told you we pretty much knew what we wanted to
do with everything. The girls were clear-cut in what they
wanted, what they didn't, and that has made it easier on me.
But there was one thing everyone was in agreement
on…and that was that they wanted you to have something
special."

Claire pulled back, flattered and surprised. "Your mother
did more for me than I ever did for her, Hunter."

"I know you think that, but—"

"No, I *mean* it," she emphasized.

"Still. You were there for her, and she could depend on you.
We all recognize that. Every one of us, and we appreciate it."

"We were just here for each other, that's all," Claire said
softly. "If I needed advice she'd give it. If she needed something from the store, I'd pick it up for her. That's all. It was a
very good arrangement."

"Even so, we wanted you to have something." He turned
over the envelope, and pulled the flap free. "It's sort of from
all of us, but mostly from me."

"Okay…but…" Claire dubiously considered the envelope,
uncertainty seeping through her. "I didn't expect this. Really."

"That's what makes it all the better." He pulled the sheaf
of papers out, then extended them, folded, to Claire. Her gaze
quizzically collided with Hunter's. "Go on," he urged. "Look
at that, not me."

She wanted to object and say that was all she needed, to merely look at him. For today. Tomorrow. For a lifetime. "There's an awful lot of papers here," Claire said awkwardly, fumbling to unfold them. She tried to make sense of them, but her thinking was muddled. "This is…" She scanned the notarized copy.

"The cabin," he said softly. "You always loved it. I wanted you to have it."

Air whooshed from her lungs. "What?" She looked at all the signatures, from the paperwork, to Hunter, and back again.

"The cabin," he repeated. "For all you did for my mom. And for all you did for me." He laughed. "You gave me a helluva childhood, Claire."

Her muscles went marshmallowy, and she could barely breathe. With her hopes fading, her defenses rose in the core of her, to protect her and save her from one last hurt.

She'd given him a helluva childhood, but she wasn't woman enough to give him a helluva life.

The deed blurred before her eyes. "No. I'm sorry. I—I can't accept this."

"Claire…?"

Panic gripped her, making her want to stuff all the papers into the envelope and shove it back at him. "You can't just give me—a—a piece of property!"

"But we spent so much time out there. As kids, friends—" his hand crept over to cover hers, and she knew he felt her shaking "—lovers." He squeezed her hand. "Come on. It's okay," he urged. "Really. I want you to have it. I bought out my sisters' interests. With their blessings," he added proudly, "because I told them I was deeding it over to you."

Silence loomed, crackling like thunder off the walls. She pulled her hand away and tried to concentrate.

"Hunter. Listen to me. I can't accept this."

"I know you didn't expect it, but—"

"No. I didn't. A canned ham, maybe. A gift certificate, possibly. But your family's cabin? The place where we…we got in so much trouble…and swam in the creek…and…" *Made love that first and very special time?* "I can't," she said flatly. "It's too much."

"It's a gift. For you. Because you always loved it."

She concentrated on folding the deed back up and putting it in the envelope, but her hands were shaking so much that she struggled to make it fit. Finally, she slid it across the table toward him. "No, thank you. I can't."

Surprise and confusion rippled over Hunter's features. For the briefest second, it looked as if he'd been slapped. "Claire, a man tries to give you a gift and—"

"This isn't a gift, Hunter. It's a payment."

"A what?"

"You're trying to buy me off."

"I'm…?" He slammed his fist on the table. "Oh, for—"

"I didn't do those things for your mom, thinking I'd get something in return. I didn't do anything for you, thinking you needed to thank me. Or that you owed me."

"I spent three days getting everything in order!"

Awareness of where he'd been the last three days trickled through her. He'd been wasting his time, putting together something she couldn't possibly accept. "I'm sorry. I'd rather have had those three days with you. Because accepting a gift like that is completely out of the question."

"What?" he demanded. "Why?"

Claire stalled. How could she possibly tell him that cabin didn't mean anything if she didn't have anyone to share it with? If he wasn't out there with her? That she'd never be able to go out there again without thinking of him? "I can't, Hunter. It's too much."

"Why do I get the feeling this is personal?"

"Because," she said softly, "it is. I can't help but wonder if you're offering it to me because of guilt."

His eyes flashed in her direction, and his head imperceptibly turned. "Excuse me?"

"Guilt," she repeated. "Maybe you think you owe me. I have the feeling this is your way of paying me back, of making up for all those promises you couldn't keep. For a marriage you couldn't go through with."

His jaw slid slowly off center, then tightened, snapping back into place. "Claire. Listen—"

"I can't help feeling that way."

"Well, you're wrong," he declared.

She looked away, gnawing on her lower lip. "It's the way I feel. And, yes, I love that place. I do," she admitted, sadly realizing she could say that she loved some place, but that she couldn't say she loved *him*. "I've got plenty of memories out there. But I refuse to taint them with reminders of everything we couldn't have together. I couldn't possibly go out there, thinking that this was your way out, the way you could leave with a clear conscience, or—"

"Oh, dammit, Claire! Get off it! I didn't mean it that way," he said, his voice rising. "God, it never even occurred to me you'd think—"

"How could I possibly go out there and not think of you?" she interrupted. "Our lives were intertwined out there. In every intimate way. We played in our diapers in the old washtubs your mom filled up for us. We grew up out there…and we made love out there. From innocence to intimacy."

His mouth thinned, and his smoldering gaze slipped over

her, as if he were momentarily reliving the joyous, sensual interludes they had once shared. He'd discovered every secret place of her physical body, and she'd wantonly let him. It had been so right, so perfect.

"You were an incredibly passionate young woman, Claire," he said finally, huskily.

"And I gave you everything, Hunter. Everything."

Hunter grew silent. His jaw jutted slightly forward, and the vein near his temple throbbed.

"But I'm not that kind of person, Hunter," she said. "I never cared about your money then, and I'm refusing to accept your extravagant gifts now."

"Extravagant gifts!" he scoffed, sliding the heels of his hands to the edge of the table and pushing back. "Trust me, this isn't extravagant, Claire," he denied, sweeping an arm through the air as if he could, if he chose, give her the world. "If I wanted to impress you with extravagance, I'd sweep you off your feet with indulgences and not even blink an eye or feel the sting in my wallet. It's a rustic, run-down old cabin with a view. That's all. It'll probably cost you more than it's worth," he grumbled, settling back against the chair. "I wanted you to have it because I knew how much it once meant to you. I wanted to include you in our family's inheritance, in our legacy. You're the one trying to make it into something else."

"No. You don't get it," she argued. "I don't need gifts. Because there was only one thing I ever wanted. One." She lifted a finger and aimed it at his chest. "And that was you. *You*," she emphasized, the single word ripped from her throat, from the very bottom of her soul. "I can't be bought, Hunter. And I refuse to sell my dreams for a pittance. Certainly not for a piece of property that has all kinds of broken, beat-up memories attached to it." She picked up the envelope and extended it. "Here. Take this home with you. Because I can't accept it."

Hunter distinctly remembered how he'd grabbed the envelope and stomped home with it. He even remembered thinking, as his feet hit the driveway, that he was acting as if he were twelve and Claire had refused to help him with his homework. He'd tossed that envelope on the table as if it had been junk mail.

Then he'd yanked out a chair and sat and stared at that envelope as if it was a big, ominous thing that had taken on a life of its own.

He'd find a way to make her accept it, come hell or high water. It was nothing but a crummy little house surrounded by land that couldn't be farmed because it was cut up by two creeks, limestone flats and a bunch of gnarly, broken-down trees. Why, in Claire's line of work, the cabin would be referred to as a fixer-upper.

A part of him hadn't been joking when he said it would probably cost her more than it was worth. Forget the potential, most people would have bulldozed it by now and started from scratch.

Still…he knew—and his heart kept reminding him—that the cost to her wasn't financial. It was emotional. Claire saw things others didn't see. She felt so deeply, so intrinsically, that her emotions were simply another play in the mix. She probably was being honest when she said she had too damn many memories tied up in the place.

Okay, he grudgingly allowed, maybe the gesture had been stupid. He hadn't thoroughly considered the emotional ties; he'd only thought of how that place had once made her eyes light up and her cares fall away.

He'd only meant to do something good for her. It wasn't a payback, and he didn't do it because of guilt. It wasn't his intention to buy her out or buy her off. But he guessed he'd never convince Claire of that.

Old prideful Claire—she'd turn it down on mere principle. Why, that girl would shoot herself in the foot, just to make a point. It wasn't rational to turn down a gift worth thousands and thousands of dollars.

It wasn't!

She was one complex, contrary, ornery woman, that's what she was.

Damn it all to hell! She needed to grow up, distance herself from the whole mess and realize what that cabin was worth. Why, the acreage alone was a financial investment. With that resort going in out near the lake, the damn thing could be her future, not her past.

He drummed his fingertips impatiently on the table.

Okay, all right, he'd confess. He'd be honest—even if it was only with himself. When he'd been lining things up, it had occurred to him that once he was gone he'd feel better knowing Claire would have more security, or even a retreat. But, maybe as Claire accused, those had been his own selfish dreams. To ease his conscience. Or, to make him feel as if he'd done the right thing where she was concerned.

He hated to admit it—but he could see how she could view it that way.

He didn't want to think it was guilt…yet as he sat there and eyed that damn envelope his subconscious needled him. He'd wanted to do something for her. But he wasn't sure what, or even how to go about doing it.

He couldn't give her what she wanted most—to tell her that he still cared about her—because he didn't know how he felt about anything anymore. He'd lost his mom, and he'd put his work on hold, and now his sisters were looking at him, expecting him to make the right decisions, to shoulder the responsibilities for the estate and family. He'd never been one to shirk, and he didn't intend to now, but everything seemed overwhelming. From the dozens and dozens of salt and pepper shakers his mother had collected to the safe-deposit box of stocks and bonds and titles and deeds he'd unearthed. He was finding all kinds of surprises.

And Claire was one of them....

She was every little bit that he remembered...and everything more. She was a deadly combination of fascination and frustration. She'd grown into a woman with softer, curvier sides and a knowing smile. Each moment he spent with her made him wonder what he'd missed, what had made her this way, what had sculpted her wit, her strength and her determination. He wondered, too, if she'd have been the same person if he'd stayed.

He wondered, vaguely, if he kissed her again what it would lead to.

Hot, hungry sex, that's what.

Maybe that's why he hadn't kissed her. Because the spark was still there, hot and sharp, with a bite that would lead him straight into her arms and a tumble into bed.

He couldn't risk that. He couldn't. He feared if he did, he'd never be able to let her go.

He'd come back to Lost Falls thinking he was in charge, in control, and that he knew it all. But Lost Falls had a way of getting under your skin. And the people in it—including Claire—made an impression that you carried with you always.

Now he only knew this: He had set out to make something of himself and he'd succeeded. He had a home and a life waiting for him in California—not in some down-home, out of the way Wyoming niche. And certainly not with a woman who was determined to stay there.

Chapter Nine

Claire hadn't slept a wink all night. She wiped a hand over her tired eyes and glanced at the clock in the office, wondering if she should just give up and go home. But she couldn't bring herself to do that because she risked running into Hunter. It was better to stay here and lie low. To avoid him, at all costs.

She couldn't believe she'd turned down his offer of the cabin last night. Then again, she couldn't believe he'd offered it to her.

She *loved* that place. It had been her safe haven. Even after Hunter left she had gone out there occasionally for quiet time, to consider what they'd shared and to appreciate the incredible beauty and the exhilarating isolation.

What she should have done was offer to buy the cabin. Not that she could have afforded it, but she should have made the offer. It would have been a far more gracious way to turn Hunter down. Rather than coming at him with her nostrils flared, making accusations about guilt and history and owing people things they couldn't possibly make up.

She didn't know what had gotten into her.

The three 'Ls', maybe?

Lust, longing and love?

It could have been very simple, really. He could have given her the deed, and she could have thanked him, but said it was too generous. She'd offer to buy it from him and he'd name a reasonable price. Then she'd say she needed a couple of days to get the financing together and could have come back later confiding that she'd thought about it and didn't want the responsibility of owning another place. Simple as that. Case closed. No harsh words, no regrets, no looking back.

Now Hunter would probably never want to see her again. He'd most likely nod curtly and keep walking if their paths ever crossed again.

Claire sighed and pushed back from her desk to make a copy of the listing she'd stared at for the last two hours. It was time to quit rehashing her pie-in-the-sky dreams and disappointments and get back to real life. That's what paid the bills.

The hinges on the screen door creaked, and Claire glanced up just as Hunter stepped inside the front door. She plopped back in her chair, her heart pounding. Everything faded from her peripheral vision.

The soles of Hunter's shiny loafers rocked on the threshold. The screen door rested on his shoulderblades. "You busy?" He didn't offer a greeting, he just asked.

"Actually, I—" she tapped the listing she'd been unable to focus on all morning "—I have a client who is determined to find a larger home in the next few weeks. I'm working on that."

"Oh. Well. Can I come in?"

"Of course. I—" she swiveled the chair a quarter of a turn, to face him "—I've been thinking about you."

He nodded. "Mmm. Me, too. Thinking about you, that is."

Claire took a shaky breath, convinced he was going to light into her for being ungrateful and rude. "About what I said last night..." Hunter's gaze strayed to her broker's—Jo's—closed door. "She took an early lunch. So she's not here right now," Claire hastily explained. "Actually, Jo and Rich aren't here most of the time. They've sort of given me free rein to keep this place going." Claire paused, hesitating. "Um, about last night? Could we just forget it ever happened? I overreacted. It was generous and thoughtful of you. I just—" She helplessly lifted both hands. "I..."

"No. Don't. No apologies." He tilted his head. "I know why. I do. It took me a while to think about it. I expected a certain reaction, and when I didn't get it..."

"It was a generous offer," she repeated. "But I wouldn't feel right about it. I'd feel like I was taking advantage of you. And—"

"Claire?" he interrupted, taking two steps into the room. "Forget it. It was a misunderstanding on both our parts."

Relief washed through her, and she tried to laugh. "I figured you went to bed mad and woke up offended."

"I did. And I was." His step was determined as he crossed the room and slipped into the chair opposite her desk. "For a little while."

"I knew it."

"But I got over it." He propped his elbows on the arms of the chair and sat forward. "It isn't like we haven't had our disagreements before."

Claire looked away uncomfortably. The pose he struck was so masculine, so inviting. His shoulders bunched. His forearms were broad and tanned and sinewy. The dark hairs on the back of his hand were visible and the blue veins were raised, weaving an intricate pattern beneath the flesh. "Yes. I know," she said, her voice barely above a whisper. "But…I felt bad about this one."

Silence echoed through the room. Then a car honked outside, and the fax machine behind her started spitting out paper.

"Claire. I did come here to talk about the cabin. But not the way you think."

"Okay…"

"Well, I bought my sisters out. Now what am I going to do with it?"

"It might be a nice place to come home to," she suggested carefully. "I mean, you *do* take vacations, don't you?"

He snorted. "Don't know the meaning of the word. I take working vacations."

"Some kind of tax write-off?" she queried. "You could rent it."

"That's a possibility," he allowed. "But I know the cabin needs work. Mom said the roof leaks and there were raccoons under the porch last year. I imagine the whole place should be rewired. Probably would need to be replumbed, too. And my best guess is that it's so overgrown with weeds that it'll take a machete just to hack a path to the front door."

Claire choked over a laugh. "My. And this was your gift to me. Why, thank you. You've made it sound like you want to unload an albatross that's hanging around your neck."

The beginnings of a smile teased Hunter's mouth, making it tilt sexily to the side.

The dimple popped out on Hunter's chin, and he levered himself forward. "That's why I'm here. I want you to list it."

"What?"

"I realized it's the thing to do."

"Oh, Hunter, no. That cabin's been in your family for—what?—fifty years? Your grandfather built it, piece by piece. He spent all his time out there. It may be a little rundown, but you grew up out there. All of you. Surely someone wants to see that it stays in the family."

He shook his head, and a glimmer of sadness rolled through his eyes. "Claire, the girls aren't interested. They hated it. They always complained there was nothing to do. They complained about the bugs and the mice. All the *creature* comforts of living in the country, they said."

"But…they have *little boys*," she pointed out, her mouth wistfully churning out the words. "Little boys who would love to play in the creek and fish in the lake and make trails through the woods, and—"

"Beth's six year old wouldn't last five minutes out there. He's got allergies."

"He's not the *only* one who would benefit from—"

"They all live too far away. No one wanted to be bothered with it. Not even me. Only because I live too far away, too. But I knew you loved it, so…"

Claire's eyelids briefly shuttered closed. She didn't want to get into that argument again. "Okay. Maybe take a year. Think about it, then if you still feel the same, if they still feel the same…" She couldn't keep the pleading from her voice. "I mean, so what if it sits for another year?"

He hesitated. "Claire," he said slowly, finally, "things change. Sometimes they're just over."

They looked at each other, neither of them saying anything.

"Of course," she said stiffly, "I understand." But she didn't understand. Not at all.

"So if you'd list it for me…"

"Me? I'm not the best one to do this," she said, uncomfortably.

"Why not?"

"Because my memories may get all mixed up with value," she reluctantly admitted. "It might be better to work with Jo. She could give you a better idea of what it's worth. Like I said, she's rarely here anymore, but I'm sure she'd take on the property if I asked her."

Hunter gazed at her shrewdly, and for a moment he said nothing. "I value my memories, too. But I'd rather list it with you."

Claire waffled. He was asking her to negotiate a contract and ultimately say goodbye to something that represented the best years of her life. "Something like this...it would throw us together all the time."

"So? I trust you," he said flatly. "In every way that counts."

She sighed, wearily thinking of all the implications. "Hunter, listen to me. Friends and finances don't mix. When it comes down to money—"

"This isn't about the money."

"But it's my job to worry about a client's investment."

"Great," he said spontaneously, as if her statement had clinched the deal. "Because you know the place better than anyone. You know every little quirky aspect of that cabin and the land around it. You're the best possible person to show the property. I want to list it with you, Claire. Only with you."

Hunter knew full well he'd badgered Claire into taking the listing. He'd also persuaded her to go out to the cabin to look it over. They were six miles out of town, on Highway 51, and he kept looking over at her on the other side of the car and thinking how much of a ruckus she still caused with his hormones. There were moments he felt as if he were sixteen again.

He was supposed to be thinking about taking room measurements and how far he'd be willing to go to fix up the place. Instead he was thinking about how her face had filled out, into the gentlest of curves. He'd look over at her hair and think of the night they'd spent in the backyard, how the moonlight had highlighted her crown and glistened like dew across her cheeks and the slim column of her neck.

The hard lemonade he'd offered had loosened her up, making her voice seductively low, reminiscent of silk slipping over satin. A mysterious aura had hovered over her that night…and he thought about it now, unable to get it out of his mind. He wanted more of it.

He saw the sign for The Spur and took his foot off the accelerator. "You hungry?" he asked. "I know you missed lunch because of this."

Claire turned to face him and, with the window half-down, her hair floated around her like spun sugar. "That's okay. I can pick something up later."

"C'mon. Let's stop at The Spur."

"Well…" Indecision darkened her eyes, putting a curious hitch in his groin. He'd seen that same expression years ago, when the physical wanting was more than either of them could handle. "I haven't been there in ages," she said finally. "I heard it went downhill."

"They made the best bacon-and-tomato sandwich. How can you ruin that?"

"I imagine there's a way." The hint of a smile touched her mouth. "You used to live on those things."

"I know. And they used to put a half a pound of bacon on every sandwich. And I'd order two," he bragged. "Wonder what that did for my cholesterol."

They topped the rise and The Spur came into view. A few

battered cars clustered around the ramshackle café. Brown paint on the rough plywood walls now peeled until the silvery-gray weathered wood showed through. The front door was warped and hung slightly ajar, and the porch tilted to one side, as if an earthquake had repositioned it.

"They certainly haven't refurbished," Hunter said mildly. "But my guess is the food's just as good—or probably better—than I remember." He tapped the brakes, then wheeled into the parking lot, making limestone dust purl over the rear end of his car.

They jounced over the potholes, and Claire clutched the armrest. "This is going to cost you a tire," she warned. "It'll be the most expensive bacon-and-tomato in history."

He just laughed and pulled up on the far side of the parking lot, next to the splintered telephone pole where the weeds were knee-high and flourishing. "Memories do come with a price, Claire," he chided. "I'm a person who's willing to pay for them."

"You're lucky you can afford to pay for them," she said dryly.

He switched off the engine and gave her a sideways look. She'd been an indomitable spirit when she was a child, and she'd been a beauty when she was a teenager. But now there was something more, an ephemeral quality that had him in its hold. He turned and hung an elbow on the back of the seat, then reached over to tuck a strand of her hair behind her ear. He offered her one outrageous wink. "I'm a lucky man," he said huskily. "Incredibly lucky. To have had so many beautiful women in my life. My mom. My sisters. You."

He heard her catch her breath and knew he'd caught her off guard.

"You don't have to say anything," he said quickly. "I just

felt like I could say it. Because that's what I was thinking. I didn't mean to be sappy or anything."

"It wasn't sappy, Hunter. It was…special…to hear something like that and believe that you meant it."

"I did."

"I—I know."

Her voice quivered, and he had the strangest desire to kiss her. To show her that everything was right—about this moment, about the cabin and them and the way things had turned out. Without thinking, he twined his fingers through the wispy ends of her hair. "You going to order a chocolate malt like you used to?"

Her eyes warmed, and a smile eased onto her face. She leaned closer to him. "I might."

He wanted her to, he wanted the familiarity, the sameness, the knowing what to expect. But he also knew everything was different, and he had to be careful. He couldn't take reckless chances this second time around. He couldn't hurt her, and he couldn't let himself fall victim to everything that was uniquely Claire.

"It would be kind of like old times," he said finally, reluctantly pulling his fingers from her hair. "At least for one afternoon," he qualified.

"One afternoon," she agreed, meeting his gaze.

"Okay, then." He sucked in a long, cleansing breath, and immediately wished he hadn't. Claire smelled as inviting as vanilla, as warm as baby powder. He got out of the car, with the scent of her working its way into his brain. They walked shoulder to shoulder to the restaurant.

The interior of The Spur was as run-down and worn-out as they remembered. The regulars contentedly sat at the scarred tables, swatted at flies and slathered baskets of home-made bread with real butter. They called the waitress by her first name, and if they needed something from behind the counter they got up and got it.

Hunter steered Claire into the empty booth nearest the jukebox. Before he sat down, he dug in his pants pockets for change. "Got any quarters?" he asked.

Claire fished in her purse for quarters and handed them to him.

While Hunter pored over the selections, the waitress dropped off two menus and two glasses of water. "We're all out of meat loaf," she warned Claire.

"We want two bacon-and-tomato sandwiches."

"Good choice," she approved, scooping the menus back up. "You want fries with that?"

"To share," Claire replied. "And Cokes to drink. One with lots of ice and one with none. And for dessert, two chocolate malts."

It never occurred to her not to order for Hunter, or that his preferences might have changed. He slid into the booth, a grin on his face. "You remembered. Even about the ice."

"Habit," she admitted. "I guess by now, though, we could each afford a side of fries."

"Maybe. But—" he shrugged "—it's best not to mess up a good thing."

Strains of "Brown Eyed Girl" reverberated through The Spur. Claire's nerve endings came alive. He'd picked that song the night he told her he didn't want to date anyone else, only her. He'd said it reminded him of her. He must have forgotten he'd ever told her that, because she knew he'd never play that song if he'd remembered.

She turned her water glass so the chipped rim was away from her, and took an unsteady swallow of tepid water.

Hunter thumped his knuckles on the table, as if he couldn't

look at her and listen to the music at the same time. His gaze darted between the dusty beer signs and the faded checked curtains at the windows.

"Imagine this place will go under when they get that resort going out at the lake," he said finally. "Hate to see that happen. All that traffic, all those fast-food places springing up."

"Keep in mind it'll be good for property values. Ten years down the road that cabin could be worth five times what it is now." She paused. "If you'd want to wait on the listing I'd understand."

"Nah. We need to get it done and over with."

The waitress slid the Cokes in front of them. Claire took the one with ice, Hunter the one without. He used the straw; Claire took hers out and laid it aside.

"How many acres again?" Claire asked, reaching for her day planner where she kept all her personal notes about listings. "You told me, but I was so surprised that there was that much land with it, that I—"

"Thirty-seven," he automatically answered, lifting his Coke. "They lost a little when they sold the corner to the convenience store and widened the intersection." He took a drink, then added, "Yeah, somebody will buy that cabin for the land. I know it." He watched her scribble the information in her planner. "Claire? Do we have to do this now?"

"No. But I just thought..." She stopped and abruptly slapped the planner shut before jamming it back into her purse. "Actually, I don't know what I was thinking."

"Imagine that," Hunter said, his eyes crinkling. "You talking business and me not wanting to."

Claire, vaguely conscious that the song had ended, realized Hunter's second choice, one with a catchy refrain about being "down in the boondocks!" had started. "Interesting music choices," she mused. "I have the strangest feeling I'm either getting my quarter's worth or I'm getting subliminal messages."

Hunter didn't answer, but he looked guilty as sin.

Chapter Ten

The cabin was smaller than Hunter remembered. He stared at the broken-down porch railing and reminisced about how many times he'd sat on it, dangling his legs and watching the fireflies light up the darkness. Or the times he would tease Claire into the corner, then trap her and kiss her under the moonlight until she melted in his arms.

"Does it look the same?" Claire asked, breaking into his thoughts.

"Excuse me?"

"The cabin," she prompted. "You're staring at it like you've never seen it before."

"Oh. I…was just thinking."

Claire moved ahead of him and up the front-porch stairs. Her sandals tapped across the worn wooden planks. Hunter hung back.

"Look," she said, leaning over the rail on the south side, "the irises your mother planted are in bloom."

The purplish heads rose out of the weeds, swaying in the breeze. Hunter didn't want to look too carefully, because in his mind's eye he could still see his mother fussing over her gardens, arranging the rocks she'd carried up from the creek as if they were fine marble sculptures. "They're about to be taken over by weeds," he dismissed.

"We can fix that. I know someone who can clean up the yard. He's reasonable, and he does good work." Claire stepped back down onto the dusty driveway, crunching over the remnants of gravel.

Hunter waited until she joined him, then turned away to walk toward the barn. He kicked at the pieces of a broken beer bottle with his shoe. "Looks like the teenagers use this as a hangout," he said.

"Well, hey, we did."

He gave her a sideways glance. Mischievous light played in Claire's eyes, a smile hovered on her lips. He grinned. God, he was glad she didn't get all melancholy on him about being back here. "It would be best," he said, "not to talk about our own misguided youth."

Her smile widened.

He inclined his head toward the remnants of the split rail fence. "I can pretty much show you the boundaries from there."

They moved in unison toward the fence, skirting patches of flourishing weeds and kicking at bits of trash. Hunter stopped at a timber that rested on the ground, propping the sole of his shoe on it. He pointed out the things she already knew: how the creek ran through the property, the limestone flats where his father cleaned out eighty-seven—or was that eighty-eight?—snakes one summer.

He made sweeping gestures with his hands, and she stood

next to him, listening. He kept talking about whatever came into his head, but his mind was only on how Claire fit against him. Her shoulder seemed to meld beneath and against his. She turned and the sleeve of her light summer blouse whisked against his bicep.

The breeze fluttered through her hair, and she unconsciously smoothed it back.

Every gesture she made held a strange fascination. The way she shaded her eyes to look into the distance for the five pines his father had planted for each of his children. The way she lifted her face beneath the sunshine, her eyelids drooping, her lashes feathering in long spikes against the translucent flesh above her cheeks. The way she pivoted on one foot to look at the rusty old hand pump at the well.

"The trees have grown ten feet," he remarked, looking at the portion of the woods where they had once built elaborate forts.

"A foot a year. That's what they say," Claire said.

He looked up at their towering height, wondering again how much he'd missed in his last twelve absent years. "Funny. The cabin looks smaller, but the wide-open spaces make the place look bigger."

Her chin lifted, and she tilted her head to look back and over her shoulder at him. "The city will do that to you. Messes up your perspective."

Did it? he wondered silently. Because from this perspective, Claire was looking like everything he'd remembered and more. The more fool him, to walk away from her like that.

"The barn—or what's left of it—does have character."

He pushed off the fence and made a detour in the direction of the old hip-roofed barn. Claire walked beside him. "Much left in there?"

"A few pieces of rusted old machinery, I think."

He walked around to the front, tossing aside the metal pipe that had been propped against the sliding door and pushed it back. Dust motes swirled and drifted in the cavernous space. Hunter took two steps inside. "Always loved this old barn," he said, looking overhead at the patches of sky showing through the holes in the roof. "Something about the smell, and the dust, and the weathered, worn boards."

Claire followed him inside and stopped at the horse stall, running her fingers over the rusted nails his father had once pounded into the beams. In an effort to entice his girls into spending more time at the cabin, he'd gotten them a pony, Dolly. But only Claire and Hunter had doted on Dolly, feeding her, riding her, brushing her until her hair nearly fell out. They'd hung her bridle, her halter and lead on those very same nails.

And then Hunter got older and started riding bikes and playing baseball, and Dolly had gone to live with another family who had two little girls….

Claire moved away, looking up, taking it all in. "It's going to take a truckload of money to put a roof on," she said sadly.

"Mmm. More money than it's worth."

Claire took a deep breath, then pulled out a tape measure and waggled it at him. "So. Help me measure the rooms, and then we can figure out how the cabin stacks up against a 3,000 square foot town house."

"No comparison," he said easily. "I have a gourmet kitchen, two whirlpool tubs and skylights."

She turned, moving outside and into the sunlight. "And out here you've got a vegetable garden—or what's left of one— a mineral spa—otherwise known as Watson's Creek—and a canopy of outdoor lighting."

He chuckled. "Clever. I can see why your listings get the

job done." He moved behind her, letting her lead the way back up to the cabin.

Claire didn't walk. She strolled up the path, her fingertips trailing over the tops of weeds, her attention fixed on passing butterflies. Hunter moved in beside her, putting his hand on her waist, pulling her back from stepping on a rusty tin can.

"Whoops." She faltered, staggering against him.

"Your sandals," he said, his arm looping her waist. It struck him right then how Claire was warmer and softer than any woman had a right to be. He tried to sound offhanded, warning, "Strappy little shoes like that are going to get you in trouble out here." But the kind of trouble he was considering had nothing to do with a tetanus shot for stepping on a rusty tin can.

"I'll have to watch where I'm going," she murmured.

He didn't know why he did it, but he kept his arm around her waist. Part of him wanted to make a show as if he was protecting her, but the other part simply ached to touch her, to hold her. They walked that way, another forty tormented steps to the cabin's front door, and he had to finally, reluctantly, pull away to fish the key from his pocket.

"Have you been inside since you've been back?" she asked softly.

He inserted the key into the old brass lock, then turned his head to glance at her. "No, I figured I'd let it go as is."

The door swung open and the musty stale smell of disuse rolled over the threshold. He reached inside to flick the switch, surprised the overhead light hadn't burned out. Everything was just as neat, just as worn as his mother had last left it. Pieced quilts hung over the back of each of the threadbare wine-colored chairs. The hideaway, flush against the far wall and flanking the fireplace, had a pillow on one end and two raggedy stuffed animals on the other. The checkerboard and checkers had been left on the small corner table, and jigsaw puzzles were stacked on the floor next to it. A motley collection of bud vases littered the mantel.

"The decorating leaves something to be desired," Hunter observed.

Claire walked across the room and examined a few of the bud vases. "I'll bet I filled everyone of these with wildflowers at one time or another."

He knew she had.

They walked into the kitchen and stopped short at the huge picture window and the rolling vista beyond. The massive square table had always been in the same place in front of it; eight sturdy, mismatched chairs around it. His family had always joked that the eighth chair had Claire's name on it. He regarded it now, suddenly aware of how well she had fit into his family.

"Kitchen's pretty rustic," Claire commented, taking in the pot rack, the two-burner stove and the badly chipped sink.

"Mom had the money, I don't know why she didn't modernize it."

"It wouldn't have been a retreat if she had. This way she couldn't get bogged down with cooking big meals or making excuses for using paper plates."

Hunter ran a hand over the cracked linoleum that had been glued over plywood for a makeshift countertop. "My grandfather did this," he said. "He loved to make do."

"Ah, but he didn't waste the view. Not with that picture window."

"He sure didn't." He pointed to a low spot, near Watson's Creek. "He used to have a salt lick down there, and we'd watch the deer. Remember?"

"I remember you played Robin Hood one whole summer, certain you'd get a deer with your bow and arrow."

He lifted an apologetic shoulder. "My aim wasn't so good."

She snorted. "Frankly, I was kind of glad."

He reluctantly moved from the window to the hall and the connecting bedrooms. But Claire puttered around the kitchen, feigning interest in the small refrigerator. She looked up and saw him waiting, and the guiltiest expression crossed her face. "Um, if you want to go ahead…"

"No, that's okay. I'll wait."

"We could measure these rooms."

"Okay."

So they did…and then there wasn't anything left to do, but go forward and step into the rooms where they had once experimented with passion and the soaring power of love.

Hunter pushed open the door of the master bedroom. They stood in the hall and stared with bated breath, taking it all in. Logs were laid on the grate of the fireplace, a quilt folded at the foot of the high double bed. The dresser had glass drawer pulls and ornate carved legs. The mirror was hazy, offering up smoky, distorted images.

Neither one of them said anything. Finally, Claire pulled out the tape measure, more because she needed to keep her hands busy than because she cared whether the room was twelve by seventeen. She silently offered him the end. After they took the dimensions, they each turned away, silently, thoughtfully going their different directions.

Hunter moved to the fireplace, kneeling down to flick a finger over the remaining ash in the hearth. Claire moved to the dresser, where an old oil lamp stood on a yellowed crocheted doily.

"It's still romantic," Claire said, her voice dropping to a reverent whisper. "It's like something out of the past."

On the ball of his foot, Hunter swiveled, studying Claire.

"You once said all that romantic stuff was made up and hokey."

"I was wrong." She traced a corner of the doily with her fingertip. "I was a kid, what did I know?"

He sat back on his haunches, his forearms resting on his knees, his hands dangling between the V of his legs. "I thought you knew everything. You were a bright, articulate…passionate…young woman." Claire's gaze drifted in his direction. "I mean it," he confirmed. "You were all that, and more."

She took a shuddering breath, and her blouse vibrated against the tops of her breasts. "And now, I'm…"

"Incredible."

"Hunter—"

He stood before he could verbally interrupt her, but the truth was he didn't want her to say anymore. He didn't want to think about anything, he just wanted this moment. With her. He crossed the room in two great strides. "I wish you'd reconsider," he said. "I see you here. You love it so."

She shook her head and tossed the pad and pencil on the bureau. "I can't. I…"

"Claire-bear," he soothed, "don't." She was going to choke up, and he wouldn't be able to tolerate that. "I understand. And you're right. It'll probably be best for both of us this way." He started to chuck her under the chin, as he'd done when they were in grade school…and then he paused. With the tip of his finger he caressed the soft flesh beneath her jaw, tracing a path forward to tilt her chin up. He didn't ask, he didn't explain…he just did it.

He lowered his head and brushed his lips over hers. Then he kissed her softly and with every bit of compassion that was left in his battered, confused soul.

It almost surprised him that she didn't try to pull away. But, he guessed, she needed this as much as he did. Her long, slim body fit against his. Her breasts molded against his chest, her arms embraced him, and her hands slid up over his upper arms and shoulders until her fingers inched to the back of his neck. Their legs sluiced together. Thigh to thigh they swayed.

He deepened the kiss, and his mouth tasted. His tongue probed. She met him halfway and he recognized the faintest flavor of chocolate and spearmint. Heady sensation throbbed within him, numbing all rational thought.

On a physical level, his reaction was immediate. He was hard and ready, and instinctively moved in the direction of the bed.

Claire simply clung to him.

Her heavy, accommodating body moved with his. Like a flash it struck him that he couldn't take it to the next step. All of his yearnings ground to a halt, like a machine shutting down. He reluctantly pulled away, breaking the kiss.

"Claire-bear?" he whispered. "You okay?"

Claire struggled to focus, and she felt her eyelashes flicker. She felt woozy all over. The unexpected, spine-tingling kiss had done more than unnerve her; it made her realize that she'd compromise just about anything to have Hunter back. Even for a little while.

She straightened, her arms falling from his neck, his shoulders. A cold gust of air tickled her middle, where the buttons had popped free on her blouse. She self-consciously tugged at them, but her fingers were too numb to close the gap.

"I didn't do that," he said quickly.

"I know. It's the blouse. It does that." She swallowed convulsively and smiled awkwardly, ashamed to realize that she would have let him lead her to that bed. She shivered.

"Claire? You okay?"

"I…didn't expect that."

He hesitated. "Me, either."

"It's probably being out here again. Seeing all the old familiar things." She tried to shrug, but couldn't quite manage it. "With you."

"I know. Kind of knocked me for a loop, too."

She turned away, but felt his hand go to her elbow. "I should have come out here by myself like I suggested. That would have eliminated all these goofy feelings."

"Vulnerable feelings?" he asked.

"Oh, great." She rolled her eyes. "Is that what I look like now? A vulnerable woman?"

He hedged, avoiding the question, "I don't know. Being out here kind of put a soft spot in me."

She moved away from his grasp to stand in front of an old collection of framed photos on the wall. "This place, it does have its memories. I'll give it that."

"Claire? You're not mad? That I kissed you, I mean."

She silently shook her head, and her fingers tightened around the tape measure. It was ironic that she had been holding it when she kissed him. "I'd rather not talk about it," she finally said, swiping up the pad and paper she'd discarded. "I think we've done enough damage today."

He nodded and followed her outside, locking the door while she kept her back to him. When she heard the lock click into place, she slipped into her Realtor's demeanor. "I recommend you have someone mow and pick up the trash. It would help to paint it and fix it up, but I'm not sure it's really worth it. There's so much to be done."

"I know." He stood beside her, shoulder to shoulder, on the front-porch step, his hands in his pockets.

"The place looks…loved…as it is."

He snorted.

"Look, Hunter, I need to do some comparisons with places that have recently sold. But here's what I think it's worth." She jotted a figure on the paper and handed it to him. "I could be off five thousand either way."

Hunter stared at it and said nothing, then, "Up it by fifty thousand."

"What?" She looked up at him, startled. "It will never sell. Not at that price."

"So? Being out here has made me realize I have all the time in the world. I really don't care, and I'm not in a hurry."

Chapter Eleven

The kiss didn't mean anything. It was a nostalgic gesture, that was all. At least that's what Claire told herself as she put everything in order for the listing.

But she couldn't erase the memory of how Hunter had moved toward her, his fingertip gliding along her jaw, his lips softly claiming hers. His warm breath teased, and the stubble on his cheek scraped. Their bodies instinctively gravitated toward each other, straining to be as close as possible. Her thoughts had been irrational, but there was one thing she remembered—she hadn't been able to get close enough. She'd wanted all of him. She'd wanted to make love to Hunter, and afterward wake to Hunter's even breathing, to his head on her chest, to his arm draped possessively over her middle. She could imagine all of it happening in the cabin where they'd first made love.

And then he'd broken the kiss and looked guiltily away. She thought he'd even apologized. But she couldn't remember. Not exactly. She'd said something stupid about her blouse, and he'd vehemently denied unbuttoning it. But it was the strangest thing. She wished he had. For she ached, literally ached, to be touched by him.

Pushing the anguished thoughts from her head, she stared at the photos of the cabin. They had turned out far better than she'd imagined they would. The outside views portrayed an idyllic setting; the inside shots made the cozy rooms seem charmingly rustic. It was breaking her heart to let it go—and she couldn't fathom how Hunter could indifferently attach a huge price tag to the property and walk away from it.

But that was what was happening. The listing would go into the next issue of the local paper. She'd gone out alone yesterday and put the sign up. She'd made arrangements with Jim to keep the property mowed and to clean up what he could.

They were moving toward a sale, and—damn—she hoped Hunter wouldn't try to kiss her when she found a buyer. It would be more than she could tolerate.

She looked up just as Hunter rounded the corner, a cardboard box in his hands. Claire stilled, pushing the photos of the cabin to the back of her desk.

He shouldered open the screen and grinned. "You *are* here."

"I usually put in a full day. But—" she suspiciously eyed the box "—it makes me a little nervous to have you stop by the office twice in one week."

"No reason to be nervous. I come bearing gifts." He sidled around a table, then plopped the cardboard box on the corner of her desk. "I could have dropped these off at your place, but I couldn't wait to see what you thought. Look." He pushed back the flaps on the box and drew out a framed photograph. "That's you and me in Mrs. Updyke's room. For that Valentine's party? Look, you're wearing your snow pants under your dress."

Claire winced. Her ankles were wrapped around the rungs of a tiny chair, making her snow pants pop out like two loaves of fully risen bread dough. There was a construction-paper heart pinned to her chest and a hair bow the size of a decorative wreath stuck to the back of her head. "Thanks for noticing my fashion statement, but that's probably not my most glamorous pose, thank you."

"But it's cute. You look so happy."

"Cute? I'm wearing a heart the size of Texas on my chest because I won the Valentine's box."

"I know. I've got two copies of the picture, so I thought you'd like to have this one."

"Really? I can have it?" She accepted it eagerly. She had so few pictures of her childhood; her mother and father hadn't bothered with things like that.

"Mmm. And that's me. There. Behind you."

"Oh, I saw you. Peering over the hair bow."

He laughed. "And look at this…" He took a huge rusty horseshoe out of the box, wiped a little dirt off of it and laid it on her desk. "We each got one when we went out to ride the horses at Cal Mosely's place. Remember?"

"They had the farrier there that day, and he gave us each a horseshoe to go away and leave him alone." Claire smiled at the memory and absently traced the inside curve of the horseshoe. Cal, Hunter and Claire—maybe ten or twelve at the time—had hung on the fence, pestering the poor man until he'd bribed them with the horseshoes.

"You probably don't want it, but—"

"No, I'll…I'll keep it if you don't care." Claire's horseshoe had mysteriously disappeared. Either one of the boys had run off with it, or her mother had slipped it in a trash bag.

"I don't care. What am I going to do with it?"

"Actually, I think you're supposed to hang it over a doorway, upside down, to catch all the good luck. Something like that. And considering what you want to ask for the cabin, you're gonna need all the luck you can possibly get."

He gave her a dry look. "Don't deviate," he admonished. "I'm on a mission here. I've unearthed all these neat things in the attic." He pulled out an old autograph book. "Look. It's yours. I don't know how we ended up with it."

"You were supposed to sign it and never brought it back," Claire said simply. "I kept hounding you about it, and you said you didn't know where you put it."

"Probably forgot all about it," Hunter said, dismissively, rummaging through the box again.

Claire flipped through the pages, recognizing the familiar names of school chums, pausing to read the goofy rhyming words. Then she stopped cold at the next to last page. It was signed by Hunter, age eleven. Scanning the words, she knew why he'd "lost" it and hadn't had the courage to return it to her.

Claire and Hunter sittin' in a tree.

I like her and she likes me.

First comes love, then comes marriage

Then comes Claire with a baby carriage!

"And then there's this, Claire," he went on, oblivious to her find. "I'm not sure if it works, but you can have it if you want. The girls always thought it was butt-ugly and none of them wanted a thing to do with it." He offered up the old chiming clock his mother used to set in the window, to remind them of when it was time to come in.

Claire quickly closed the book and put it aside, her heart pounding. "I wonder if it still chimes," she commented, popping the latch on the glass face, her mind on the autograph book and the revealing poetry Hunter had written.

"I don't know. But my mother hated that clock. She said she used to wish it would fall out of the window and break so she wouldn't have to guard it with her life. It was a wedding gift that my Aunt Bess asked about all the time."

Claire chuckled, imagining Ella trying to pacify her mother's cantankerous sister. "It is rather…unique."

"Ah, carefully put."

"But it did make beautiful music."

"Take it. Hock it if you want, it may even be worth something. And—" he peered into the box "—there's some other stuff in here. Take what you want. I've got so much stuff to sort through I don't know what to do with it all."

"Garage sale?"

"Forget that."

"Auction?"

"Nope. Mom always said she didn't want folks pawing through her stuff. She'd rather give it away."

"Well, then, Lost Falls is having their Summer Social in a couple of weeks. You might give everything you don't want to them. All the monies raised from the white elephant sale are going to go to purchasing land and developing a playground for the community."

"Really?"

"Mmm-hmm. I doubt Ella would say no to that. It's a good cause and you could get rid of a lot of the little stuff that way."

He debated. "Will you help me sort through it all?"

"What?"

"You'd know better what would be appropriate. And then, if you wanted anything—or ran across something you thought one of the girls might want—you could pull it out. I feel kind of helpless with all this stuff. Like a fish out of water. I mean, the attic's full, the closets are stuffed, the basement is piled with boxes." He leaned closer, confiding, "I think the girls knew what they were doing and got out with their lives."

Claire laughed.

"If you'd just help me send it in the right direction," he coaxed. "There might even be a few antiques and stuff and I wouldn't even know it."

"Well…I suppose I could spare a few hours."

"Tonight?" he asked hopefully. "After you get off?"

In spite of her best intentions to refuse anything that had to do with Hunter Starnes, Claire agreed.

Hunter put the last bag in the car and stood back, surveying the mangle of bags and boxes. "You sure that isn't too much? Because I can see we could have at least two more trips after this one."

"No. Barbara said they'd take all they could get. Last year they didn't have enough donations and had to put things out sparingly."

He glanced over at her. "You're coming along, aren't you?"

"Well, I—"

"Come on. We'll stop for ice cream on the way back."

"You're bribing me. Probably because you want another warm body to help you unload."

"Warm body?" His gaze appreciatively flicked over her. "Be careful. Shouldn't go loosely throwing terms like that around. Gives a man ideas."

Claire rolled her eyes, let her jaw slide off center and shook her head. "You missed the point," she said.

"Mmm." He went to the car door and held it open for her. "Maybe, maybe not. I think I just read a little more into it."

There it was again, Claire thought, sliding into the interior of Hunter's SUV, all that simmering sexual innuendo. She never knew when he was kidding anymore, and the not knowing made her skittish.

They had spent five days together cleaning out cupboards and boxes and closets and the work hadn't been grueling, it had been fun. They had laughed together and discovered together. There were poignant moments that had made them put their heads together and left them in awe. Memories to be cherished, moments to savor. They learned more about Hunter's family than they'd bothered to find out when they were growing up.

It had been good. Therapeutic almost, for both of them.

Hunter climbed in beside her and switched on the engine. He backed out of the drive and headed over to Barbara's. They were a block away from her home when Hunter began slowing the car. "Claire? Thank you," he said. She turned to look at him. "If it hadn't been for you, I still would have been floundering around with those 167 pairs of salt and pepper shakers."

"I don't think so. You're a businessman, you know how to make decisions."

"Maybe. But this time around it's been different." He squinted, peering down the street for Barbara's house.

"The one with the green shutters and the three-car garage," Claire directed.

Hunter passed the drive, then backed into it. As if on cue, one of the garage doors lifted and Barbara, a spry fiftyish widow, came out of the house. "Hi guys!" she sang. "I was looking for you."

Hunter switched off the ignition and got out. "Hunter," she exclaimed. "You look great! I'm glad you stuck around Lost Falls long enough to make a few donations."

Hunter nodded at Claire. "It was her idea."

"Doesn't she always look out for everyone's best interests?" Barbara wrapped Claire in a quick hug. "Claire, thanks for sending this boy my way. The playground committee thanks you."

Barbara helped them carry everything into her garage and waved a hand at the dozens of banana boxes stacked against the far wall. "I mark everything and then we take it over to the tent during the Social."

"So what do you all need for your project?" Hunter asked ten minutes later, after he set the last bag on the floor of the garage.

"What don't we need? A shelter. Picnic tables, benches. We may decide on a downtown lot after the Social."

"You don't have one then?"

"No, this is still a long overdue idea. Your mother said we needed to do this years ago. She was right." She glanced fondly at Claire. "And Claire's managing the food tent this year."

His forehead furrowed. "Claire? You never said anything."

"It's not a big deal," she said. "I'm setting it up, and Ron Johnson is tearing it down. I got the easy job."

"Claire always helps," Barbara confirmed. "Last year, she organized the parade."

"But I only did it because the real estate company sponsored a float," Claire explained. "I didn't stand on the float. I didn't wear a fancy dress or do the princess wave—" she mimicked the stiff, cup-shaped motion with her hand "—I just lined everybody up and sent them on their way."

Barbara inclined her head, confiding, "Don't believe her. She worked on it for months." Barbara paused and took a step back as if she were sizing him up. "So? How about you, Hunter? You're going to be around for the Social, aren't you? We need some workers. Can't let Claire get the best of you and get all the attention for her good works. Not when you're a strong, able-bodied man. It would be a shame to have you stand around doing nothing."

Hunter opened his mouth, as if he was working his way around an excuse.

But Barbara didn't give him the opportunity to offer it. "I've got just the booth for you. Say you'll do it."

"I'm really better with donations." Hunter's hand moved to his front pocket, as if he was searching for his checkbook.

"No, no. You can't get off that easily with me," Barbara chided, clucking her tongue against the roof of her mouth. "Donating your time is just as important."

"You'll be here for the Social, won't you?" Claire asked.

"Most likely."

Barbara lifted both hands, palms up, as if that settled the matter. "You'll have fun and see people you haven't seen in ages. You've got to work the Social, that's all there is to it."

"But I don't have any experience in fixing food, or organizing parades, or—"

"I've got something you can do…." Barbara trailed off.

"Go on, Hunter," Claire urged. "Do it. Say you'll help."

He hesitated, then agreeably muttered, "Oh, all right. Sign me up."

Barbara clapped her hands as if she'd just made a coup. "The kissing booth! You'll be perfect for it. We'll set you up on Saturday night and I guarantee the line will go all the way around the block."

Claire gasped, and her stomach turned over. She hadn't seen this coming—and apparently, from the look on Hunter's face, neither had he.

Chapter Twelve

Claire dumped another batch of hot dogs into the cooker and cast a furtive glance in Hunter's direction. It was pretty much as Barbara had predicted. The line for one of his kisses trailed out to the corner of the block. At least it wasn't all the way *around* the block. If it had been, the man wouldn't be fit to live with.

Not that *she'd* ever live with him.

Claire winced, watching Hunter paste Liz Howard with a mind-boggling, gut-wrenching, toe-curling kiss.

Who did he think he was, she thought hotly, some Rudolph Valentino?

For cryin' out loud, *her* toes were curling—and she was standing over a pot of boiling water in the food tent on the other side of the sidewalk.

Claire watched Liz wriggle her shoulders and arch her spine, as if Hunter's kiss possessed the power to rearrange her inside her skimpy little sundress. Then Liz gazed up at him, her mouth in a sexy little pout, her adoring eyes fastened to his. She must have said something provocative because Hunter grinned.

Claire glowered and indignantly ripped open a bag of hot dog buns and pulled them apart. He'd actually leered at Liz Howard. Leered! He'd never leered at her like that! And he'd kissed her—what?—three times since he'd been back.

What was she supposed to do, pay to have him spout a little of that smoldering heat over her?

Liz still stood there. Still holding up the line. Still talking to Hunter. The woman had the audacity to laugh. Then their heads bobbed together, and she reached over and patted him on the forearm!

Claire saw red. She couldn't tear her eyes away, and she couldn't concentrate. Liz Howard had just copped a feel! It didn't matter that the point of the charge was below the elbow and above the wrist. Or that Hunter had subsequently turned his arm over and frowned at his watch. It was unbearable. Simply, positively unbearable.

Wrapping the twist tie from the bag of buns around her finger, Claire realized she'd never be able to look Liz Howard in the eye again. Knowing Liz, she'd probably stroll right over to the food tent, sidle up to Claire and have the temerity to ask if Hunter had been that hot of a kisser in high school.

Pulling the twist tie tighter, Claire sized up the remainder of Hunter's eager ladies-in-waiting. Sally Stover. Beth Cline. Judy Wilcox. Marilyn DeVries. Roberta Culver. Tracy Cisneros. Maryellen Booth…and at least six others she didn't know.

Criminey, you'd think the women of Lost Falls had never laid eyes on a red-blooded, sexier-than-sin male—let alone gone lip-to-lip with him.

The timer went off on the hot dogs, and Claire jumped. So

what? Let 'em boil another minute. Just as she was doing. Sinking back on one hip, she looked at Hunter Starnes, wondering where the heck she'd failed.

As if he knew she was watching him, he looked over, caught her eye and winked. Then he waved. Happily. Very, very happily. She wanted to wipe that grin right off his happy chops.

But Claire controlled herself, and with the empty bread wrapper still clutched in one hand and the twist tie cutting the circulation off her forefinger, she waved back. She probably looked more as if she was issuing an SOS rather than a greeting. But Hunter never noticed—because he had turned his attention to fulfilling Sally Stover's wildest fantasies.

Sally, with her high-heeled cowboy boots and her swaying waist-length hair, was anything but shy. She wrapped her arms around Hunter's neck and drew him right down to her gooey lip gloss.

"Gimme me a ride, cowboy," she purred.

Hunter felt his eyes widen, but reined in his surprise. It wouldn't do to overreact, not with Claire giving him the eagle eye. He intended to play this role to the hilt, and he refused to disappoint Claire. "Sally?" he asked suggestively. "You aren't wearing your spurs, are you?"

Her laugh was deep and rich and throaty and she pulled him down for a smacker. Not much of a kiss, Hunter thought dismally, but he tried to give her her money's worth.

She cackled when she let him go. "Whoooo, doggies! Now that had a little kick!" she declared, loud enough for Claire to hear.

He squinted a look over at the food tent, and a feeling of satisfaction rolled through him when he saw Claire furiously jamming hot dogs into buns, then smashing them into their foil wrappers.

She was all worked up and in a jealous snit. That did so much more for his determination to carry out the charade.

Hunter kept working, knowing that both of their shifts were supposed to be done at eight. But he noticed she took her apron off early and disappeared. After that, he simply went through the motions. Smile and kiss. Smile and kiss. It was rather like an assembly line, really, if you thought about it.

Or didn't think about it.

Thanks to the street band revving up on the next block the line began to dwindle. He was down to five minutes and two kisses. Then Claire slipped to the end of the line. She'd touched up her lipstick—some sexy shade of persimmon and peach.

His heart started hammering and his mouth went dry. Not good, not for a man who had volunteered to pucker up and do his civic duty. He exchanged pleasantries with the last two ticket-bearing women. Then the world faded, and he was face-to-face with the woman who knew every intimate detail about his kissing.

He leaned across the high counter. "All I've got left is a two-for-one special," he said, letting a suggestive note weave through his words.

"What? You used everything else up?"

Hunter chuckled. "Pretty much."

"Mmm. Well, that's okay, because I don't have a ticket. I'm used to getting freebies."

"Ahh. Well. Hate to break tradition, then," he said smoothly, leaning closer and letting his gaze dip to the mustard and ketchup speckling the front of her shirt. "You smell sweet, like relish."

She imperceptibly backed away. "I have absolutely no intention of being part of that germ warfare, Hunter. I didn't come for a kiss."

"You didn't?"

"Absolutely not. Why, one more and you'll probably suffer a stress fracture. Your lips must be black-and-blue by now."

He threw back his head and laughed. "You sound positively jealous, Claire-bear."

"I am not."

"Yeah. Right. Should have seen the look on your face when Barbara said she'd put me in the kissing booth two weeks ago."

"I didn't look like anything," she denied.

"Claire. You've been looking all night. And you've been simmering ever since."

Claire's lower jaw slid off center. "Okay," she conceded, "the few times I *did* look over here, it looked like you were enjoying yourself."

He arched an eyebrow. "Volunteer work is a trial and tribulation, but someone has to do it. So I want you to know I just put a smile on my face and toughed it out."

She wrinkled her nose and started to turn away, but Hunter caught her. His fingers captured the fine bones of her wrist and drew her back to him. "I saved the best for last, Claire," he said huskily, his voice dropping to an intimate whisper. "For you."

Her mouth parted slightly, into a tiny little O of shock and surprise. Hunter intentionally made the moment last. Overhead the strings of colored lights flickered as the other workers in the booth dropped the striped canvas sides to close up shop. But Hunter kept on working…and the others smiled knowingly at each other, and let him. He dipped his head to Claire's, possessing her with his gaze, while his hand, on the small of her back, lifted her to him. His mouth brushed over the softest, sweetest part of her. He tickled her nose with his, then playfully nibbled her lower lip. He began with a blissfully sweet kiss. But instinct and longing took over, and the kiss became passionate, seductive.

Everything spun out of control and the background noises matched the fireworks in their heads. The warm comforting scents of cotton candy and warm pastries only fueled their desires. The throbbing beat of the street band matched their growing pulse.

Reluctantly, Hunter pulled away. "I think I've got a problem."

"Hmm?" Claire leaned dizzily into him. "What?"

"I think I shortchanged the other customers. Damn. If they saw the kiss I just gave you they'll want their money back."

Claire's shoulders convulsed and she buried her head against Hunter's neck. He heard a giggle escape and gave her a hug. "You aren't mad, are you, Claire-bear? I was just doing my duty."

"I'm not mad."

"I told you I saved the best for last. Come on, I'm done and I'm outta here…." Over her head, and with one hand, he worked the ties on the striped tent covering to let his side down. Then he let her go and met her on the other side.

"So that was the best you've got, huh?" she asked.

"Nope. Those were the preliminaries. You know the hayrack ride that's sold out? Well, I got two tickets. From Liz Howard."

"From Liz?"

He nodded. "She said you worked too hard and needed a little fun." Tossing an arm around her shoulders, Hunter steered her in the direction of the park.

Claire hung back, her expression bemused. "Liz said that?"

"Mmm-hmm. After she scalped the tickets for twice what she paid for them." He grinned, remembering how she'd haggled over the tickets at the kissing booth. "But I figured they were worth every penny."

Claire let herself be led to the pickup point for the hayride. She was quieter than he'd seen in a long time, and Hunter guessed she was tired. She had knocked herself out helping him at the house and working on the Summer Social in between. They waited on a bale of hay, thigh to thigh, until Ed Vanderbeek's old John Deere rolled into sight. He pulled a fancy hay wagon and it was piled high with loose straw.

Hunter handed him the tickets and directed Claire to a cozy spot in the back corner. The sun was just beginning to set and the air to cool.

"Probably should have brought jackets," Hunter muttered, as he hunkered down beside her, burrowing into the straw. He casually slung his arm over her shoulders. "Unless you're adverse to me keeping you warm."

"I imagine I can stand it."

Hunter winked, then nodded to old acquaintances. The hay wagon filled up and Ed climbed up on the tractor. He turned back on the tractor seat to make sure everyone was seated, and the ticket taker had offered last-minute instructions about keeping all hands and legs inside the wagon. Then Ed opened up the throttle and the wagon pitched forward.

Claire lurched, knocking against his ribs. The hold he had on her shoulders tightened, and the same old protective instinct he remembered from his youth welled. He leaned closer to Claire's ear, nuzzling the wispy strands of her hair away. "Remember the hayride we had in tenth grade," he asked, "when Eddie got too close to the ditch and turned the wagon over?"

"You felt it going, and we jumped. Hand in hand," she replied, her expression softening.

"That was a rush, wasn't it?"

"Yeah, I guess we've had our fair share of fun and excitement."

Hunter nodded, content to look up at the overhead canopy of maples, the darkening sky. A few minutes elapsed, and as they left the lane and moved into an adjacent pasture stars began highlighting the blue-black sky.

"You warm enough?" he asked, skimming a hand over her bare upper arm. Goose bumps followed in his wake, and he rubbed them.

She nodded and cuddled a little closer, moving under his arm. His lips twitched, and he ached to smile. This felt so good. So incomparably good.

He was with Claire again. And it felt right.

"You know, Hunter, we've spent a lot of hours together the last few weeks, but you haven't told me much of anything about living in California," she said. "Or your work."

"You want me to bore you to tears? Now?"

She nodded again, looking at the sky. "Tell me what it's like."

"It's busy. Traffic everywhere. And fast-food places on every corner. It sometimes takes me an hour to drive five miles. Here it would take me five minutes."

"And you gave all this up, for that?"

"I've got a town house with an ocean view. Well…" he revised, figuring he ought to tell her the truth, "it's an ocean view if you look between two other buildings and over a bunch of rooftops. If you stand just right on the deck, you can get a glimpse of it."

She laughed. "You, of all people, Hunter. I can't believe you left the wide-open spaces to be squashed into humanity. For a bird's-eye view of the ocean?"

He arched an eyebrow. "You might be right. I don't know what I was thinking. Especially on a night like tonight."

Claire seemed pleased that he'd said that before she looked away.

"And your work?" she asked.

"It's…well, work." He paused, thinking of everything that had happened in the last ten years. "I met the one right person and wangled a deal, and after that everything fell into place. I made more money than I ever dreamed of. I brushed shoulders with people I once read about."

"It doesn't surprise me, Hunter. I always knew you'd be successful. At whatever you chose to do."

He picked up a piece of straw with his free hand, running his thumbnail over the end of it. "You were always my cheerleader. You always believed in me." Claire's eyes crinkled at the corners, and her mouth lifted. "When I told my folks about my ideas, they'd smile and nod—and I knew they were just indulging me. But you believed me. You always believed me."

"That's what friends do, Hunter," she said softly.

"We've always had this friendship that transcends all else." He leaned his head back and sighed, thinking about how deep their friendship had been as kids. "Okay. Listen up. I'm going to tell you something I never told anyone else."

"What?"

"You know those years a kid goes through when he can't stand girls? I think it's fourth or fifth grade or something like that?" Claire frowned, but said nothing. "I never once considered you as one of those silly, annoying, prissy girls. It was like you were set apart, different from all the rest. And remember that time all the boys went out to Jimmy McEntee's for that swimming party, and everybody made a big deal out of it?"

Claire's eyes narrowed. "You stayed home, and we spent that day at the cabin. Because your mom wanted us to help her fix that broken window in the barn."

"No, she did that because I said I wasn't going to go. Not if you weren't invited." Claire's lips parted in surprise and her lower lip quivered. It occurred to him then that he'd never seen a mouth more inviting. More kissable. And he'd seen an awful lot of them in the past few hours. "It wouldn't have been any fun, Claire. Not if you weren't there."

She blinked and looked away. "I can't believe you're telling me this. Now. After all these years."

"Didn't seem important then. It's just the way it was. But, now? For some reason it seems important for you to know."

"We've always been friends, Hunter."

"Except for these past few years when we let things slip."

"Yes, well…"

"I'd kind of like to pick up where we left off, Claire. About being friends, and all. I know you've got your life and I've got mine, and I know that we may not be headed in the same direction. But I'd like to be able to call you when I want to, and stop over when I feel like it. These past few weeks have made me realize how much I've missed talking to you."

"I think we've both missed that, Hunter."

He hugged her tighter and flung the straw away that was in his free hand. Then, putting the pad of his thumb to his tongue, he offered it up. She pressed her thumb against his and they sealed it with the "twist," the one that carried them through childhood and adolescence. Then he smiled broadly and laced his fingers through hers.

It felt as if he'd been given a reprieve and everything inside him began to unwind and relax. Tension drained from his shoulders, and his mind cleared. He no longer felt there was a price tag attached to everything he said and did. He could be himself. With Claire.

She was his friend…and he hadn't had one of those in years. She was someone to whom he could confide his deepest secrets, his most intimate thoughts and his most candid fears. She was his safety net. She was fiercely loyal and undeniably dependable. She was devoted to him—and he regretted that for too many miserable years he'd foolishly turned his back on her.

Her only flaw, he reminded himself, was that she'd never leave Lost Falls...and his life was invested—heavily invested—elsewhere.

Chapter Thirteen

Claire couldn't have made a pot of coffee if her life had depended on it—and she needed one good, strong cup. She hadn't slept two hours in the past twenty-four. Her mind was in a whirl, and Hunter was smack-dab in the epicenter of it all.

She'd laid out her best intentions to forget him. Now he wanted to talk? He wanted to call and drop by? And along the way he just wanted to exchange a few hugs and fond kisses?

She wasn't up to it; she simply wasn't.

The kiss at the kissing booth had left her weak. The intimacy and romance of the hayride had undermined all her denials of affection. He'd held her hand, and her world went wild with expectation. She felt appreciated and treasured—and loved.

She hadn't felt loved, not like that, in a long, long time.

Maybe she should chuck it all. Tell him that she'd give up everything—her job, her home, her life—and go back to California with him, if that was what he wanted. For she didn't think she'd be able to endure being a long-distance friend.

Right at this very minute—at 9:18 on a Sunday morning— she'd do just about anything to have him back. She'd tromp over to his house, rouse him out of bed, sell her soul and have mad, uninhibited sex with him. She'd promise him the moon. She'd give him every last ounce of her strength, her ambition, her love.

But she wasn't sure any of it was enough. Nothing she had to offer and everything she'd become couldn't compete with his business and the world he'd created for himself. She knew that. Hunter and all he'd accomplished was bigger than she could possibly begin to be. She was no match, not for any of it.

She'd told Hunter she'd meet him promptly at one o'clock this afternoon at the band shell in the square. He claimed he wanted to enjoy the last few hours of the Summer Social, to kick back and get ice cream and be there for the closing ceremonies. But he was so specific about all of it that she had the feeling he had an ulterior motive…and she was eager and torn just thinking of it. She had less than four hours to get ready, and she knew it wasn't enough time.

Yet, at 12:59 in the afternoon, she had on her white eyelet summer skirt and matching blouse. She'd worn her favorite pearl-drop earrings, bracelet and sapphire ring. Her hair was done up, in a romantic knot at the back of her head, with tendrils curling at her nape and from her temple. If this was the first day of the second half of her friendship with Hunter, she intended to make sure he remembered it.

Claire immediately spotted Hunter and did a double take. He was sitting on the dais, proud as you please, between the mayor and the president of the Summer Social.

She stared at him, then sought the nearest chair, stumbling over the feet of the mayor's wife to get to it. She sank into the gray metal folding chair, then turned beet-red and apologized all over herself.

"Are you okay, dear?" Mrs. Mayhew inquired solicitously.

"Fine. I'm fine," Claire mumbled, unable to tear her gaze away from Hunter.

"And doesn't your young man look nice, sitting up there?" she said.

"He's not my young man."

"Excuse me, dear?"

"He's…my friend."

"Of course, dear." Mrs. Mayhew reached over and patted her hand. "And he's such a generous young man."

Claire's head swiveled, wondering what in the world the woman meant. Donating a few knickknacks to the white elephant sale had never earned her a spot on the dais. Neither had organizing the parade. Or working the food tent.

The ceremonies started immediately. Fortunately, they were brief and to the point. Hunter saw her and nodded, and then, when the crowd had swelled and people were standing on the perimeter, he was introduced. He moved to the podium with the aplomb of a politician, offering up his most brilliant smile. Adjusting the microphone, he took control.

"Ladies and gentlemen," he began, "I want to thank you for including me in this year's Summer Social. Being here, seeing everyone again, has brought me back to my roots…and I've discovered that's a pretty good thing. My mother loved Lost Falls. Most of you are aware that in her last years she traveled the world, but she was really the happiest when she returned here, to her home. I had the good fortune to learn recently that the monies raised from the Summer Social will go to playground equipment, for an as yet undesignated park and playground. However, on behalf of my mother, in her memory and as a symbol for her love of Lost Falls, my family and I have chosen to bequeath two acres on Cascade Avenue to be used for this endeavor." A collective gasp went through the crowd; Cascade Avenue was one of the most desirable, beautiful locations in Lost Falls. "My parents purchased those lots years ago, intending to build their dream home on Cascade—but my mother later confided to me that she was living her dream, and she was home, right where she was, with her family, her neighbors and a lifetime of happy memories on Maple Avenue. I know that she would be pleased that generations of Lost Falls residents will benefit from her gift to the city. Thank you for giving me this opportunity to make all of our lives richer."

Thunderous applause followed Hunter's speech. Claire, stunned, clapped only because those around her did. While she'd always known Hunter's family was comfortable, they'd never flaunted their good fortune. Certainly, no one in the community expected the children to give a portion of their inheritance away.

Of course, no one would have expected Hunter to offer the cabin to Claire, either.

"Come along, dear," Mrs. Mayhew invited, standing when the ceremonies concluded, "let's go get our men. There's still a full day of the Social to enjoy."

Claire followed Mrs. Mayhew, then hung back, watching Hunter glad-hand people he didn't know and accept hearty claps on the back from those he did. He was besieged by friends and well-wishers.

As the crowd began to disperse, his golden gaze fell on her. A light breeze gusted, making her skirts billow, the hem brushing against his pant legs like an invitation.

"Well, don't you look nice," he said.

"Mmm. And aren't you full of surprises," she returned coquettishly, tilting her head.

He grinned, as if he'd just done something extraordinary.

"I couldn't tell you," he whispered, enveloping her in a hug. "I thought you'd figure I was just giving everything away."

"The thought occurred to me."

"But I think Mom would have approved, don't you?"

"I think…" Claire said slowly, as he released her, "she would have been proud of you. Seeing you up there. Seeing what you've chosen to do for the community."

"It isn't just for the community, Claire. Some of it's for me, too. Because a part of my heart will always be here, ingrained in this life."

Claire leaned into him, wishing with her whole heart that she could make him love it as much as she did, make him want to commit as much of himself to Lost Falls as she did. If only wishing would make it so….

"I need someone to celebrate with, Claire. Can I take you to dinner tonight? I've got reservations at the Coyote Grill."

He was asking her for a date, Claire thought, flummoxed. Between falling all over Mrs. Mayhew and being totally blind-sided by his invitation, she felt like a twit. "I…"

"Say yes," he persuaded. "I've got tickets for the Ferris wheel and quarters to spend in the game tents. We could run into friends and just hang out until dinner."

A whole afternoon *and* an evening with Hunter? "I haven't hung out in a long time."

"Good. Because neither have I."

Claire knew that tonight Hunter was hers. All hers.

She didn't know how it happened. She and Hunter were back on familiar footing. They called each other frequently and commiserated about everyday events. Once again, they seemed to know what the other was thinking—as if mental telepathy had come into play.

Yet there was one thing they didn't fully address: their growing desire and attraction for each other.

They skirted around it. Hinting at sexual awareness. Indulging in the verbal foreplay that preceded a relationship. Tempting looks. Taunting touches. Skirmishing too close to some invisible, unidentifiable line. Pushing that line. Avoiding it. Cautiously shrinking from it.

Nice shirt, Claire-bear. Kind of provocative, that little lace tie-up thing. Those skinny little straps.

You noticed?

Pretty hard not to.

It was just so hot today. Can't get a breath of cool air.

Yeah. Sultry.

Yet neither of them had been talking about the weather, and Claire knew it. She was so aware of him her senses were razor sharp. Her nostrils flared the moment she saw him, instinctively questing for a whiff of his delectable aftershave. Her palms itched, begging to touch the muscled definition of his shoulders, his arms, his belly. Her ears perked up, memorizing the rumble of his laughter or the inflection of his favorite expression. *Swe-eeet. Hey, girl, watcha doin'?* Her tongue tingled, wanting to lick the dribble of foam from the corner of his lips after he took a long draft of beer.

All of it was driving her crazy! It was driving her insane! She wanted him so much she'd started thinking about simply inviting him over to share her bed. A simple, sensible, straight-out request.

We've known each other for a long time, Hunter. But there's one thing missing from our relationship—the physical part. I think it would meet a need for both us.

Maybe, if he agreed, she could get him out of her system.

BOOKS MAKE THE GREATEST GIFTS

PV# 0034663

XXXXXXXXXXXXX8752 VISA	9.36
TOTAL	9.36
PENNSYLVANIA 7.0% T	.61
SUBTOTAL	8.75
02 0373124473	4.50
01 0373197535	4.25

REL 7.7/1.06 43 11:48:58
SALE 5066 103 4663 01-31-05

B O R D E R S   E X P R E S S

Maybe, if they both behaved like rational, mature adults, she could get over him.

Maybe for a few dizzying minutes, she could feel sated. Fulfilled.

Two weeks after the Summer Social, late on a Tuesday afternoon, she saw him out in the driveway, washing his car. It was a scorcher for June, the heat hovering in the nineties. Hunter was bare chested, wearing nothing but cutoffs and sandals. Water ran in rivulets down his flat stomach, putting a washboard effect through the dark coarse hair. He held a hose in one hand and his hands were slightly pinker than the rest of his tanned body, his nails chalk-white. Soapsuds pooled at his feet.

She'd left the office early and had slipped into an old pair of shorts and a tank top. It took her three minutes to make the lemonade, and three seconds to kick off her shoes. She shouldered out of the back door carrying two sweating glasses. She lifted one and raised her eyebrows, as if that was the only invitation he was going to get.

"Hey! Now you're talking. Set them over there," he directed, nodding at the patio table, "and come help me."

She turned her back, and he immediately squirted her with the hose. She arched, the lemonade sloshed, and he laughed. She plopped the glasses aside and whirled. Water played at her feet.

"Gonna make you dance, Claire-bear."

"Hunter Starnes! Don't you dare get me wet!"

"Double dare me," he provoked. "See what happens."

"Hunter. I mean it. I came over to do something nice for you and—"

He jerked the hose, making it squirt all the way up her middle, stopping just short of the button on her shorts. She screamed and took two steps back. His grin went lopsided and inched up his face. "Gotcha."

"Not funny."

"You really ought to be wet all over, like me. That'll cool you off. And it's a hot day, you'd enjoy it." Hunter felt himself getting hard all over. He hadn't intended to make a wet T-shirt contest out of a little horseplay, but seeing Claire in those short shorts was getting to him. She had the sexiest legs…and he remembered good and well how they felt wrapped around him.

In a dozen years she'd sure managed to fill out in the right places, too. The skimpy little top she wore accentuated her full round breasts, and lately, he'd been almost delusional, thinking about how soft her breasts must be, how well they'd fit into his palm.

He'd played out enough scenarios of late. Mostly on how to get her into his bed. He'd considered early-morning coffee and catching her when she was still in her nightgown. He'd considered midnight drinks and late-night conversation that could be settled on a couch…or a bed. He'd even thought about inviting her for a moonlight swim out at the lake.

Yet being here with her like this, with fifty feet of hose and an endless water supply was just as good as anything. It was clean, impulsive and incredibly seductive.

He squirted her again. "Oops. You may have to change your shirt," he said. "I think I got it all wet." Pinching the fabric between her fingers, Claire gasped and pulled the soggy T-shirt from her middle. Water dripped onto her bare toes. She grimaced and twisted the front, wringing out the water. "Or…you could just lay out on the chaise, watch me finish the car and let your shirt dry."

She looked up at him from beneath lowered lashes, still

twisting the water from her tank top. "Yeah. Right. Me watching you watching me, is that it?"

He lifted a shoulder, then offered her one outrageous wink. "Something like that, honey." He turned the nozzle on the hose off. "Look. Why don't you come in and dry off? I can finish the car later."

"Me? Interrupt a man who is bonding with his vehicle?" Claire flirtatiously rolled her eyes. "I don't know…."

He grinned and tossed the chammy in a bucket of clean water. He was just ready to saunter over to where she was standing, pick her up and carry her in the house when his cell phone rang.

Dammit, not now, he fumed. He stopped, indecisively. Finally, he pivoted on the heel of his foot and jerked the phone off the window ledge, jamming it up against his ear. "This better be important," he growled.

"Hunter? Is that any way to greet the finest business partner on the face of the earth?"

"Adam?"

"Hey, man, what's up? And you better say not much, because I need to talk to you about that complex we've got going in Sacramento. There's going to be some problems with the zoning."

Hunter sent a furtive glance to Claire, guessing this call was going to cost him a whole lot more than he'd bargained for. He'd already felt the mood change. The electric spark had faded and misgivings were setting in. He could see it in the way Claire held herself, in the way she wiped her toes on the damp grass. She'd sobered, her luminous eyes going thoughtful, introspective.

Adam just kept talking.

Claire picked up her lemonade and turned her back, feigning extraordinary interest in the backyard and holding her shirt away from her middle. She took a sip, then jiggled the glass so the ice cubes rattled against the glass. He put his hand over the mouthpiece. "Claire?" She turned around. "Listen. I may be a minute. This is business."

Her carefully arranged face toppled with disappointment, and he wished to hell he could have choked on the word. Business had always come between them, in one form or another.

She set the glass down. "That's okay," she mouthed, backing away toward her own back door. "I should know by now that business always comes first with you. Look, I'll just get the glasses later."

Hunter winced. His business partner couldn't have possibly known what he'd just interrupted—or how the importance of their project faded in significance to Claire's retreating figure.

Once Hunter had walked out on her life, now she was walking out on his. Claire, with all her cool poise and savvy, had just made a statement—and gut instinct told him it was one he could live to regret.

Chapter Fourteen

Hunter stood on the front porch and gazed out into a Lost Falls morning. The air was damp, sun drenched. It was so clear he could have—if he'd crawled out onto the roof—seen for miles. As it was, he settled for looking across the street and watching Mrs. Hart hang clothes out on the line.

Wednesday morning, and she was hanging T-shirts from the hems. Some things in Lost Falls were predictable. Like the way Tommy Wilkerson always bought a paper on the way home from work, or the way Sam Beaumont always washed his windshield each time he filled up.

Hunter had never appreciated that kind of predictability when he was growing up—and lately he'd begun to wonder why. A certain comfort could be found in marking time by the seasons or familiar daily routines. In California, the seasons pretty much stayed the same, and he marked time with appointments and deadlines.

Odd how he'd lived in Lost Falls for over twenty years and

never recognized the opportunities. Over the past few weeks, he'd come to see them quite clearly. Lost Falls, like every other small town, was the victim of growth and a host of unmet needs. After donating that chunk of ground to the city two weeks ago, he'd realized he was in the enviable position of making a difference in the community. He knew how to put together deals, and how to make things happen. He understood the concrete side of human consumption and what the economy would tolerate and what it wouldn't.

Talking to Adam yesterday had only helped point him in the right direction. As for the deal in Sacramento, he could have cared less. There'd be a dozen more thankless deals like that.

However, putting together a deal like that in Lost Falls would be significant. He'd read every article he could find about the huge resort going in out at the lake. Initially, he didn't seriously consider the impact on Lost Falls. But suddenly uninvited ideas kept cropping up in his head, and he wondered if he could make them pay, if he could create a thriving business in the town where he'd grown up. He was definitely beginning to mull over the possibilities.

He was also beginning to mull over a lot more. Mostly about how he should have had his priorities rearranged when he left the first time. He'd struck out on his own, as if there had been a fire under him, but he'd not known then that the smoldering ash drawing him back, keeping him back, would be the unfinished business with Claire.

Claire.

Some kids had grown up with teddy bears, but he'd grown up with his Claire-bear.

God, she was so incredible. So beautiful, inside and out.

Used to be when he jogged, he listened to his Walkman, now he listened to the birds singing and daydreamed about

Claire. He'd think about something funny she said. Or he'd think about how she lapped at an ice-cream cone, turning it all around so it wouldn't drip. Or he'd think about catching her watching him with this pensive look in her eyes, as if she was wondering what they were missing from their relationship.

Well, he could tell her. Nothing. Absolutely, positively nothing.

She laughed at all the right times, and she knew what to say at the wrong ones. No one in his entire life had ever believed in him or given him as much support as Claire. She was one in a million.

So how the hell could he have walked out on her? He'd begun to think about that a lot; how he'd told Claire that it was over, that he just couldn't bring himself to go to the jeweler's to buy the wedding band. He'd left her standing by the cement birdbath in the backyard, and he had felt like the scum of the earth watching her fight back the tears. Her eyes were redrimmed and swollen. She'd had this little catch in her voice; he could still hear it inside his head. It was throaty and low pitched…and hauntingly seductive. It had stayed with him for years and years.

I've waited a lifetime for you, Hunter Starnes. But I can't go with you…and I can't wait any longer. If you leave now it's over…and someday you'll be the one looking back and regretting it.

When it was all said and done, he'd stalked off, tossed his suitcases in the back of his '85 Chevy and left on a half a tank of gas. He hadn't taken one memento of her. Not one. Not one photograph. Not one letter. Not a single gift she'd given him. Nothing. He'd done it purposely. Maybe because he wanted to see if he could get her out of his system. But more likely because he wanted to punish himself for treating her so badly.

He'd set out to become a millionaire, yet he'd passed up the greatest treasure of them all. It nagged at him, making him wonder what he could have become if Claire had been at his side.

But he'd been young and foolish. He'd set out alone—and he rued the day he'd made such a fateful mistake.

Claire had gotten up early and gone into the office to work. She'd felt rejected by that blasted phone call. She couldn't help it. She just did. Of course, she'd expected Hunter to take it. But that phone call had interrupted one of the most impetuous, impulsive moments of her life.

Business, he'd said. As if that took precedence over anything else.

Well, damn him and damn his business. She hated playing second fiddle to his business. She detested being put on hold while a new idea or a more fascinating offer came along. He'd never be able to leave it alone. Never. It would always come first.

Claire tossed the comparison study on like properties she was preparing for another client aside and decided to clear her desk. Today she craved a neat, orderly space—one that would take away the jumble in her head. She tossed a few stray pens and paper clips into her drawer, then pitched all the junk mail that had accumulated in her IN basket.

She pushed back the phone book, a box of tissues and the framed photograph Hunter had given her. Then she paused and idly picked up the photo.

Was it possible they were that young once? That they were such innocent souls? That they believed they could do anything, conquer anything? Why, they'd had dreams as big as Wyoming. Grand ideas, every one of them. Combined, their imagination was unparalleled. Claire had always thought if they were together anything was possible.

But twenty years later they couldn't even resolve their personal differences. Forget about conquering the world; their home front was a mess.

It fascinated Claire how they could talk about a problem yet each envision something completely different as a solution. They'd grown away from each other; they'd developed viewpoints that were decidedly divergent.

Like the cabin. Claire regarded the property with a rare reverence. It was a retreat that had sheltered her in her youth, and she saw it as something to be cherished and handed down from generation to generation. For her, it was a place where people shared their happiest moments—or their most vulnerable ones.

Save for that one day they had gone out to explore and take measurements, Hunter dismissed emotional attachments with the cabin. If he couldn't give it away, he expected a sizable profit. That was all. He was indifferent to what potential buyers did with it, whether they subdivided it into two dozen different parcels, refurbished it or put a palatial estate on the acreage—just as long as they met his price.

She'd thought he'd waffle when she told him she'd taken several prospective buyers out to look. But he didn't appear affected or even regretful. He only wanted to know what they thought was wrong with the place.

Hunter would always consider how he could do some project bigger, better. It was as if his mind worked that way naturally.

Maybe it was a brain deficiency, she thought wryly.

He'd never stay in Lost Falls because there weren't enough opportunities to motivate him, not like in California. Hunter equated amassing cumbersome bank accounts, properties, stocks and bonds to a child's board game. He may not be playing with paper money anymore, but he still loved the challenge, still thrived on the game.

He'd become a wealthy man, but he'd worked hard. His keen eye and scrupulous decision making had paid off. But she'd bet if she gave him five bucks, a pair of worn-out jeans, and a broken-down truck, he'd still exude the same integrity, still shoulder the same confidence. Hunter would remain generous to a fault—but he'd always put a price on things. He'd always want to know what things were worth.

And sometimes, she thought sadly, you just couldn't put a price tag on your assets. You couldn't measure the impact and worth another human being put on your life.

Until they were gone…and then it was too late.

The phone rang, making Claire jump. She put down the framed photograph.

"Falls Company Real Estate, Claire Dent speaking. How may I help you?" She listened to the caller's inquiry and an uneasy premonition rolled through her. This buyer wasn't a looker; he was interested. "Yes, I'm listing that property, Mr. Brubaker. The survey says thirty-seven acres. The house and outbuildings need some work, but the view is spectacular. And, frankly, I don't think you'll see a property like this come up again." She leaned back, listening as the caller explained the type of building site he was looking for. "Well, I'd be happy to show you the property, and you can see what you think. Half of it is wooded, and there's a nice little creek that runs along the back edge of it. It's very picturesque, all of it."

After he arranged an appointment to see the place, Claire hung up, painfully aware that there might soon be one less thing she and Hunter had between them.

The property didn't show well, not well at all. It started sprinkling when they left Lost Falls and by the time they were at the cabin, they slogged through a deluge. Their shoes sucked mud, their jackets were soaked. Claire fought with the umbrella, feeling a bit like Mary Poppins as she tried to point out the property lines. They eventually retreated to the front porch and discovered the roof leaked like a sieve.

Mr. Brubaker dismissed the annoying embarrassment and said he was going to demolish the cabin and barns anyway, so he didn't care and he didn't need to see the inside.

Then he made an offer that was only hundreds off the asking price.

Claire felt her heart rip right out of her chest. But she smiled sweetly and said she'd be happy to write up the offer for him, unless he preferred to retain his own real estate agent.

He said that wasn't necessary, that he trusted her. That the real estate office came with excellent recommendations.

So Claire put the deal together—and when Chad Brubaker left the office late that evening she laid her head on her desk and sobbed. Once again, Hunter was right. He'd named his price and the public rose up and met it. He was smart, savvy and—when it came to money—in tune with every commercial endeavor.

But it didn't make any difference to her if he made thousands or millions off this deal. She saw instead a lifetime of memories slipping away, right through her fingers and forever out of her grasp. She'd never get them back.

And, sadly, neither would he.

The following day, when everything was in place, and she thought she had composed herself enough to handle it, she made the fateful call.

"Hunter?"

"Hey, beautiful lady, where are you?"

His voice was so incredibly sexy she wanted to wilt. Tears welled in her eyes. "I'm at the office."

"Look, I've been trying to catch up with you. Didn't you

see the message I left on your back step? Spelled it out in gravel, just like we used to do."

Here she thought that monster SUV he drove was spitting up gravel, and she'd stepped on it, kicking it aside. "Um, no. You should have called. Or left a note."

"Darn," he said regretfully. "I suppose the rain washed it away. That was quite a downpour yesterday, wasn't it?"

"Yes, but I wasn't in town. I was out working and I got in later than I expected. So I didn't see it. The message, I mean."

She detected a slight, thoughtful pause.

"I figure I owe you an apology for that phone call a few days back." Then he chuckled. "I mean there's nothing I would have liked to do more, Claire, than give you a good drowning with the hose, but…I had to take that call. I didn't want you to think I'd abandoned you, but it was business, and—"

She swallowed quickly, unable to hear him say it again. She couldn't lose her edge. Not now. "Hunter. I'm in business. I understand what that means. You don't have to explain."

"Well, I didn't want you to think—".

"I didn't." Of course she did. "And, unfortunately," she went on, "this is a business call, too. I'd like to chat with you, but…" She trailed off, met only by silence. "Guess what?" she gushed cheerily. "I've got good news."

"Oh?"

"You've got an offer on the cabin. It's a mere $500 off the asking price."

"Excuse me?"

"Well, either we got exceptionally lucky, you're remarkably astute or I'm a crackerjack real estate agent. Take your pick. You've got a full-price offer on the cabin." Her forced exuberance was only met with silence on the other end of the line. "Hunter? Say something."

Seconds, like small explosions in her head, ticked away. "If we got an offer like that this soon, then we didn't ask for enough. I'm turning it down."

Claire's blood pressure shot right through the top of her skull. Her temples throbbed and the back of her neck ached. "You're what?"

"I won't accept it."

"Hunter? What are you talking about? You said you have no intention of returning there. You wanted me to sell it. I've invested hundreds of dollars in advertising, and I've showed that property I don't know how many times—"

"I'll pay for the advertising."

"I've knocked myself out. I've invested my time."

"I'll see you're compensated."

"You want me to call this man back and tell him you've changed your mind?"

"Claire...I have a feeling about this, and I think it's best to withdraw the listing."

Claire sputtered. "What kind of game are you playing? I can't test the market for you and have you up and change your mind when you don't think you're being amply reimbursed."

"This isn't sudden, Claire," he objected. "I just didn't want to talk about it. Not yet. I'd had some misgivings and I wanted to think things over."

"Well, when *did* you want to talk about it?"

"Claire, nothing's been happening with the property. I didn't think there was any big hurry."

"But I've been showing the property. What did you think was going to happen?"

"Claire, look… Granted, the timing's bad, but I thought it would be more prudent of me to wait to make a final decision until I got a few more things in order."

Claire slumped back in her chair. "I can't believe you're turning down an offer like this. What? You want to argue over a measly $500?"

He didn't say anything, then, "I think we need to talk about this," he said evenly.

Claire strangled over her escalating emotions, yet she had no problem spitting out the words. "No. You don't realize how hard this has been on me, Hunter. Selling that piece of property was like selling a piece of myself. You knew I didn't want to take the listing in the first place."

"I know you didn't. But you did it for me, because I asked—or because I goaded you into it."

"Try blackmail," she said testily.

He snorted. "It doesn't matter how we got here. I wanted you as the real estate agent. It made sense. No one knew the property better than you."

"Then let me tell you, I also know it well enough to know you shouldn't be turning down a gold-plated offer."

"I can't go through with it, Claire," he said flatly. "Because I'm not compromising my best interests. Not over this sale."

"You hard-headed—"

"Claire," he interrupted. "I'm not changing my mind. Not over this. Come out to the cabin and we can discuss it."

"What?"

"I'll never ask again," he pledged. "I just want you to see where I'm coming from."

Chapter Fifteen

Claire drove out to the cabin in a fury. She wondered what Hunter was thinking. Or if he was thinking. Every time she got involved with him, she discovered life boiled down to Hunter and what he wanted. His agenda. His business. His decisions. When was she going to learn?

He'd wasted her time, taken advantage of her efforts and, once again, bailed out. Without much explanation, either.

She'd had it.

Turning on her wipers, she fervently wished she could go out to the cabin one time—*this last time*—under sunny skies and favorable circumstances. Nothing that she had to say to Hunter was going to be easy but it had to be said. She simply couldn't go on this way. She was on the bad side of a one-sided relationship and it was time she recognized it.

Well, she refused to do it any longer. Flat-out refused.

She pulled into the muddy driveway on two wheels and sent an arc of muddy water fifteen feet. She didn't slow down, either, not caring whether she hit a pothole or wound up in mud up to her rims. She did regret her shoes, though.

They were her brand-new white skimmers and by the time she marched up to him in all this muck and told him what she thought, they'd be trashed. Oh, well. These shoes were made for walkin'...and that's just what she was going to do.

She threw open the car door, let it hang and squinted through the rain. The lights were on and the cabin door was thrown open. She blinked. Then blinked again. Those weren't lights....

They were candles—and they flickered from every window. Claire caught her breath, and the scent of burning wood filled her lungs, mingling with the damp air. She looked up to see smoke trail from both fireplaces. Beside the front door, a huge crock had been filled to overflowing with fresh flowers.

Hunter was setting the scene—and he'd done such a good job it unnerved her.

She moved forward. Rain spattered the shoulders of her blouse, and muddy water splashed up and onto the hems of her dress pants. The stitching on her shoes had already gone from pristine white to gullywasher-gray. Mud oozed up over the toes and heels, and water seeped into the soles, making them squishy.

She was halfway to the cabin when Hunter moved into the open door frame. He had shed his three-button golf shirt and was sporting a faded red-plaid work shirt. He wore sensible jeans and work boots.

Claire pushed forward, stopping just short of the porch. She looked up at him squarely, ignored the riot of delicate blooms in the crock and issued the first ultimatum. "You owe me a new pair of white shoes, Hunter Starnes."

His gaze drifted down to her pitiful shoes, and then he had the gall to chuckle.

"You think it's funny?" she snapped.

"I think it's the least of your worries."

All she saw was red—and it wasn't because of his blasted work shirt! "I'm not playing this game with you any longer, Hunter," she stated emphatically. "Just tell me what you want and what it will take to make you happy. How much money do you need?"

"Claire? Don't you want to come in and we could talk about it?"

"No. I do not."

"I'm not worried about you tracking mud in on the floors, if that's what you're afraid of. Hey—" he plucked at the front of the Western shirt "—I've got my work clothes on."

"The last thing I'm worried about is tracking dirt on your floors. Because my client intends to bulldoze the cabin anyway."

"Ahh." He leaned back, wedging his shoulder against the door as he mulled her revelation. "Well, looks like we've got us a problem. Because I'm not selling. There's not enough money in the world to buy this cabin. I've got my work clothes on, and I plan to fix it up."

She doggedly *thwunked* onto the first step of the porch and was vaguely aware the skies had begun to clear. "Hunter, I'm warning you...."

"Now Claire-bear, calm down. You aren't going to be out of a thing."

"I've worked on this *thing* for a month!" She belligerently took another step, pointing her finger straight at his chest.

"I'll make it up to you," he soothed, pulling his shoulder off the door frame.

"You're rootin', tootin' right you will!" She climbed the last step, moving forward as if she was on autopilot.

"'Cause I want to share it with you."

"You…what…?" She stopped, stared at him, then staggered, not sure if it was her muddy shoes or her muddled thinking. "Say that part again."

"The cabin. I want to keep it…and share it with you."

Claire's mind whirled, hoping against hope. "Share it? With me?" she repeated.

"Mmm. And I have some news for you, Claire." Her heart thrummed, her mouth went dry. "I want you to be the boss."

"The—the boss?"

"Of Falls Company Real Estate." He smiled. "Jo and her husband want to retire. I've been talking to them, and I've decided to stay in Lost Falls. I'm moving back here. I've made a deal with them and I'm buying them out." Claire's shoulders sagged in shock and disbelief. She'd wanted him back—but this was most certainly not what she'd imagined. "You'll be working for me now, but you'll need to teach me the ropes." He raised an eyebrow. "Like it or not."

"I…"

He looked at her, faintly amused. "I was hoping for more of a reaction, Claire."

"I—I think I'm having one," she stammered.

"It seemed like a prudent investment," he went on brusquely, moving out onto the porch, "to own the company. So I decided to take the plunge. There's a lot to do in Lost Falls, particularly with the resort going in outside of town. I see the potential, and I see a place for me here."

Claire could barely concentrate on what he was saying. How could she work with him, she agonized, day in and day out? Feeling as she did? Loving him endlessly, wanting him passionately. "I'm not sure this is a good idea, Hunter. Us working together. It's even worse than me taking that listing and working for you."

"What? Why?"

"Because…" Her mouth worked, but she paused, not sure she could say it. "We have a commitment problem," she said wryly, feeling a distinct glimmer of amusement for this entirely unbelievable turn of events. "You're committed to your work, and you're committed to everything you want to do. But—" she broke off "—you can't commit to me."

"Watch me."

"Hunter, I'm not talking about work. I'm—"

"I'm not, either," he said softly. "I love you, Claire."

Claire gasped, air rushing into her lungs so hard and fast it almost hurt. She swayed, and he caught her. "Could you, um, say that part again, too?" she mumbled, leaning against his chest as he held her tight.

"I love you, Claire-bear," he whispered against her hair.

"Hunter…" Tears stung the corners of her eyes, and she burrowed into his shirtfront, wiping them away, wanting to laugh and sing and make a thousand testimonials to the power of love.

"I don't know why it took me so long to just come out and say it," he admitted. "I've been thinking it for a long time. Since that first day when I came back, when I went into the kitchen and saw you. Everything was so right about you being there. So perfect."

"And I was coming out here today to tell you it was all over, the business, the friendship, all of it."

He laughed and leaned away from her to pluck a rose out of the mishmash of flowers bubbling out of the crock. He handed it to her. "There's a fire on the hearth and a flower for the lovely lady who has always had my heart in the palm of her hand."

"My, Hunter. Poetry?" she asked breathlessly, pausing to

accept the rose and drag it across her cheek, inhaling the faintest scent of it.

"Mmm. Of the homegrown variety," he said. "Nothing fancy."

"It sounded fancy to me. And something I needed to hear."

"Claire? I think it was something I needed to say." Time had no meaning as they held each other. "Honey? Would you look at that? Look up, over there." One of his hands fell from her back, and she reluctantly turned in the circle of his arms.

She followed the direction of his gaze. Clouds scudded across the clearing sky, and a rainbow, magnificent in all its ephemeral glory, shimmered. So big, so tall, so grand. The separate colors were distinguishable, and both ends seemed to reach for the sodden earth.

"Remember when—"

"—we looked for the pot of gold at the end of the rainbow," Claire finished.

They stood, clinging to each other. The strangest sense filled Claire, as if their love had been recognized, validated. "I love you, Hunter," she said thickly. "I always have, always will. I waited. I didn't mean to, but…I loved you too much to ever let you go."

Hunter's eyes shuttered closed, and his Adam's apple bobbed up and down. His arm tightened around her middle, pulling her as close as he possibly could. "And I needed to have you say *that* again," he said huskily. "I needed to know that you loved me, even after all I put you through."

She choked, nodding, turning back into him, her cheek against his chest, her ear listening to his thudding heart. His breath shuddered through his body, making his arms quiver, and his shoulders convulse. "Claire?"

"Mmm?"

"I hate to ask you one more time, especially at such an inopportune time, but…look…."

She looked up from the haven of his arms, then stared, transfixed. "A…double…rainbow…"

"I haven't seen one for years…."

"Not a full one. Not since…" She trailed off, a sense of wonder filling her.

"One for you, and one for me."

"Or…one for your mom. And one for mine."

He chuckled. "You're reaching there, Claire-bear. They got along, but they never really agreed on anything."

"Not until us."

He chuckled, conceding, "Nope. Not until us."

He angled his head down, amber light glowing in his eyes. His questing lips sought fulfillment, and Claire knew he hungered for her. Lifting herself gently up to him, she stood on her tiptoes. Then her feet left the ground.

His mouth covered hers, tasting seductively sweet, intoxicatingly spicy. She wrapped her arms around his neck, grinding the damp front of her shirt against his dry one. His arms held her securely, even as his fingers strayed onto the sensitive hollows at the small of her back, her buttocks.

Spiraling heat coursed through her, radiating outward. Conscious thought was lost. Her body surrendered to the sensations, the emotions that only Hunter could arouse. It was so effortless, all of it. So natural.

She started slipping from his grasp, and he carefully leaned forward, pausing when the toes of her muddied shoes teetered against the old plank flooring. Her weight sagged against him, and she slowly drew back, her palms sliding around his collar, her fingertips plucking at the points.

"I want to be here, with you," he said huskily, nuzzling

his chin over the top of her head. "Always, Claire. It's been a long way back, but now I know everything is right about it."

"If you think that I'm going to ask you if you're sure, you can just forget it," she quipped. "I'm taking you as is, no turning back, no regrets, no changing your mind. This is it. The final word, you know."

He chuckled. "It does seem as if all the forces of the universe are sanctioning this commitment," he said softly. "Wonder how long that rainbow's going to stick around?"

Claire sighed, fixing it in her sight. "Thirty years ago we would have been off looking for the pot of gold at the end of the rainbow."

"We still can. The rain's stopped. And you know my motto."

"Never give up," she recited, repeating one of Hunter's favorite phrases. "But this time, you have to give me credit. For never giving up on you. For waiting this one out."

He gave her hand a squeeze. "Granted," he said, nodding. "This time you win. You stuck it out. And let me say I'm damn glad you did." The brilliant colors of the rainbow began to dim. "Let's walk out and meet it," he prompted. "The rain's let up, and I think there's something that'll always be in me, wanting to find the end of the rainbow. With you."

Claire felt her smile spring from her heart, then she threaded her fingers through his. She tugged him down and onto the steps, toward the woods and the paths they'd walked as children. "The truth is, I think we already found it, Hunter."

He grinned down at her, and they strolled hand in hand toward the woods.

"Have you told your sisters you're staying in Lost Falls?" she asked.

"Not yet. But I don't imagine they'll be surprised."

"No?"

"Beth flat out told me it was time to get over myself, settle down and take a long hard look at what I wanted out of life." He picked his way around several large stones, stepping onto the path that led into the woods. "I realized I wanted you," he said, his voice filling with conviction. "More than anything else in the world."

Claire's heart felt so full she thought it would burst. "I've always wanted you," she replied. "I've always known it, and I've never doubted it."

"So I had a lapse," he conceded, walking slightly ahead of her but hanging tightly on to her hand. "Forgive me?"

"I said we weren't having regrets. The only way from here is forward."

They walked for some minutes, glimpsing patches of blue sky through the dripping wet canopy of leaves. "This used to be the shortcut to the creek, but it's so overgrown," Hunter apologized. "I'm trying to give you a picture-perfect moment, with the rainbow over the creek, but I don't know if we'll make it."

Claire looked up to see if she could see the way out, then stumbled, the toe of her shoe catching on the root of a tree.

"Watch it," Hunter warned, catching her. "You're going to get cut."

"Cut? I stubbed my toe and—" She swayed like a flamingo on one leg, bending her knee and flexing the toe of her ruined shoe.

"No, there's a rusted tin can, and…"

Neither of them said a word. Branches creaked overhead, and a blackbird cawed. Rain rhythmically dripped, plopping onto the soggy ground and layers of old, undisturbed leaves.

Hunter looked at her, his eyes wide, his expression incred-

ulous. A ripple of disbelief went through Claire, and she pivoted back to the spot where she had tripped.

"It's…buried."

"Half-buried," Hunter confirmed.

The jagged edge of a can poked through the ground, a
gnarly root rising up beside and around it. Standing at the base
of the old oak tree, Claire gazed up. The trunk was thick,
weathered. The mazelike limbs spread wide, high. "It's grown
so much that the roots have come up out of the ground…and
the dirt's been washed away," she breathed.

They simultaneously fell to their knees. Hunter clawed
away the mud on his side; Claire, heedless of the cold wet-
ness creeping through her dress slacks, pulled at the root,
prying it back. The can popped free, the upper portion crum-
bling away. Hunter wiped away the rusted tin, scrambling to
tilt the can.

They both heard a definitive *clink.*

"My God, Claire, it's still here."

A nervous laugh surged through her lungs. "No?" she
squealed, shaking uncontrollably.

"Look." He upended the tin on his open palm.

The ring, burnished a dark, coppery gold, lay in his
cupped hand.

"Grandma's," Claire breathed, filled with wonder, awe.
"Mama always wanted me to have it. But we needed the
money that year, and she intended to pawn it."

"We don't need the money anymore—and it's yours now."

Claire carefully picked it up, as if it were fragile and might
break, momentarily forgetting that this piece of gold had spent
twenty-nine years in the wilderness. But it had been forged
to last, withstanding scorching heat and freezing cold. "I got
in so much trouble…." She turned it, inspecting it.

"I think it's worth more this way," Hunter said. She glanced up at him sharply. "Because you can't put a price on it."

The tension slowly eased from Claire's shoulders. "It's priceless," she said softly.

"We found our gold, Claire. And the wealth has truly multiplied, beyond anything we could have imagined or asked for."

She laughed softly. "Look. It's engraved." She wiped at the smudges. "*M*...for Margaret. And there's more...." She squinted, trying in vain to make out the rest.

"A good cleaning will help."

She instinctively moved to try it on, but Hunter stopped her.

"Wait," he interrupted, stilling her working hands. "I think this comes with a proposal," he said. "An official one. Claire Dent, will you marry me? You'd make me the happiest man in the world. We've got the ring, and we've got the love, and—"

"Yes!" She flung her arms around his neck, the ring tightly clutched in her fingers.

He threw his head back and laughed. "Now don't lose the ring," he teased. "I don't want to have to wait another twenty-nine years to get this job done."

"I won't lose it," she assured. "And I won't lose you. Not ever again."

"It's going be pretty hard to lose me in Lost Falls. I'm not going to stray from the best part of my life. I'm going to put in my time at the office and come home early, every night, to you." He tilted his head, studying her. "You know, Claire, I'm looking forward to being a husband. Because you have a knack for making life interesting."

She basked in his praise.

"Of course, I'll have a lot to do here," he went on. "I intend to make an investment in the community, but I'll need you to help me and show me the right direction. I'll need you to tell me your ideas, and what you think."

"Well…right now, your ideas are all sounding pretty good."

He grinned. "Kind of figured you'd like 'em." He paused. "We've got a lot to do, Claire. Including finding time to have those babies." She felt a demure smile slip onto her lips. "And make 'em." He chuckled. "Now I particularly think I'm going to like that part." His hand dipped under her T-shirt, to the bare skin at her waist, and moved upward. He tickled her, his forehead suggestively lifting.

"We have a lot of time to make up for," she warned him. "But I think it all came together…just like it was supposed to."

"With a happily-ever-after commitment. I couldn't want anything more, Claire. I swear it. I promise to love you and cherish you for the rest of my life."

"I love you, Hunter." She imperceptibly pulled back, to glance at the ring, to make sure it was really, truly there. "We've got our love, and our gold—and the next time we play house it will be for real. No more tree houses. No more tents in the backyard."

He laughed. "I thought you liked primitive living?"

"Only out here."

"This is our retreat," he announced. "I have a few improvements in mind. We've got to refurbish the cabin and restore the barn. You'll want a flower garden. And I figured the kids might like a pony again."

"The kids?"

"Our kids," he clarified. "Because I imagine this place will mean as much to them as it does to us. Some things are just handed down from generation to generation."

"A whole new generation," she said softly. "From us."

"We need to get that wedding date set," he declared. "And

the sooner the better. Because I figure a good nine months after the wedding would be just about right to get started on the next generation."

She laughed, self-consciously burying her forehead against his neck.

"It's what you want, isn't it?" he pressed.

"Exactly what I want. In exactly the right order of things."

"So...? Be honest. You aren't upset about having to tell your client the sale's off, are you?"

Claire sighed heavily, feigning disappointment. "I'll find a way to get over it. But I'll probably have to go back to the cabin and rest for a while. Maybe watch the fire in the fireplace dwindle to embers, scatter a few rose petals over the bed linens...absorb a little heat, seek a little comfort. Just to get in the right frame of mind," she suggested. "Just to be able to think about what will happen, for now and for forever...."

"I have absolutely no problem guiding you through all this, Claire. No problem at all."

* * * * *

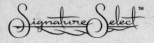

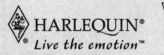

SPOTLIGHT

**Every month we'll spotlight
original stories from Harlequin
and Silhouette Books' Shining Stars!**

Fantastic authors, including:
- Debra Webb
- Julie Elizabeth Leto
- Merline Lovelace
- Rhonda Nelson

**Plus, value-added Bonus Features
are coming soon to a book near you!**

- Author Interviews
- Bonus Reads
- The Writing Life
- Character Profiles

SIGNATURE SELECT SPOTLIGHT
On sale January 2005

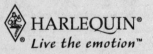

COMING NEXT MONTH

#1754 NIGHTTIME SWEETHEARTS—Cara Colter
In a Fairy Tale World...

She never forgot the brooding bad boy who had, once upon a time, made her heart race. So when Cynthia Fosythe hears a husky, familiar voice calling to her out of the tropical moonlit night she's stunned. She'd let go of Rick Barnett to preserve her good-girl image, but now Cynthia's prepared to lay it all on the line for another chance at paradise.

#1755 INSTANT MARRIAGE, JUST ADD GROOM—Myrna Mackenzie

Nortorious bachelor Caleb Fremont is just what baby-hungry Victoria Holbrook is looking for—the perfect candidate for the father of her child. Although Caleb isn't interested in being a dad, he's agreed to a temporary marriage of convenience. But when the stick finally turns pink will he be able to let Victoria—and his baby—go?

#1756 DADDY, HE WROTE—Jill Limber

Reclusive author Ian Miller purchased an historic farmhouse to get some much-needed peace and quiet—and overcome his writer's block. Yet when he finds that the farm comes complete with beautiful caretaker Trish Ryan and her delightful daughter, Ian might find that inspiration can be found in the most unlikely places....

#1757 KISSED BY CAT—Shirley Jump
Soulmates

When Garrett McCallister discovers a purr-fectly gorgeous woman in his veterinary clinic, wearing nothing but a lab coat, he's confused, suspicious...and very imtrigued. Will Garrett run when he discovers Catherine Wyndham's secret curse, or will he let the mysterious siren into his heart?